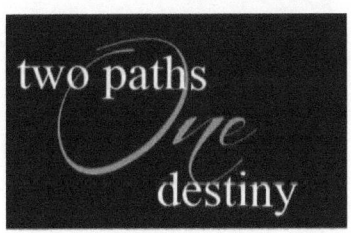

two paths *One* destiny

by Carson Mackenzie

two paths *O*ne destiny

Published by CM Books, LLC
Copyright © May 2020 Carson Mackenzie
Cover Design by Carson Mackenzie, CM Cover
Designs
ISBN# 978-1-952184-38-3 Paperback

carsonmackenzieauthor2020@gmail.com.

Synopsis

Four years of wasted time in a gang was nothing compared to what laid ahead for me—the rest of my life and what I chose to make of it. It would have been easier on me to head toward failure than to work my way out. Everything worthwhile comes at a cost—and my price was high.

Growing up surrounded by poverty was an excuse for circumstances I had not wanted to claim as my own. At least until I was smacked in the face with them. Decisions and my actions would both play roles in my success and failure.

I believe life is defined by different events that lead us to our ultimate destiny.

But what happens when events occur to two different people and cross at some point?

I am Luca Lucio Moretti, and I will give you the answer...

My life.
Her life.
Our life.

two paths *O*ne destiny

Contents

Prologue

Lucio

Karma.
Fate.
Destiny.

The first time I experienced one of them, I'd been a small, thin kid of eight. Mickey Monroe, grade school bully and all-around butthead, had snatched my skateboard and claimed it as payment for *not* beating the crap out of me. My friend, Davis, and I watched as he dropped the board on the sidewalk, jumped on, and skated away. I stood there, thought of never seeing the board again.

Then it happened.

Mickey pushed down with his back foot and tilted the board to jump the curb and instead of clearing it, the rear wheels hung. The skateboard came to an abrupt stop—Mickey didn't. At least not right away.

9

The momentum sent Mickey flying until the light pole that sat on the corner brought him to a halt—and ultimately, the sidewalk helped as he fell. When he landed on his side, the force on his shoulder and arm caused a fracture in both, and Mickey spent the last few months of the school year in a cast while I enjoyed my skateboard.

Karma: *a characteristic emanation, aura, or spirit that infuses or vitalizes someone or something.*

A simpler definition—payback for Mickey being an asshole and doing shitty things to people. Too bad it wasn't the only time I'd witness or experience karma through my life.

Decisions and my actions would both play roles in both my success and failure.

Growing up a step above poverty, a small step, was an excuse I used for circumstances I hadn't wanted to claim as my own. At least until I was smacked in the face with them.

The eye opener was the day I walked through the door of the small house where I lived with my parents and two cops stood in the living room. My eyes scanned the room and landed on my mother, who sat on the couch while her body racked with silent sobs.

"Mom?" I questioned as I moved toward her but kept my eyes on the cops while they followed my every movement. I knew what they saw and thought—a punk ass kid wearing gang colors. They were right. What they didn't see was potential, a teenager with aspirations and dreams who was caught in a downward spiral of life. It didn't matter, though. It wasn't like it was the first time I had been judged by looks alone. And more than likely, it wouldn't be the last.

My mom looked up, her face splotchy from crying, and held out her hands to me. "Lucio," was all she got out before the tears once more brimmed her eyes and ran down her cheeks. I grabbed her hands, which were cold as if she'd pulled them from a bucket of ice. Holding both within my own hands, I looked over my shoulder at the cops.

"Why are you here?" I asked, but my mom was the one who answered in between her sobs, bringing my world to a halt.

"Your dad...he was shot, Lucio. My Joe is dead."

Fate: *the development of events beyond a person's control, regarded as determined by a supernatural power.*

True for my dad that day, but the development of the event—mine to live with. And what a wake-up call for a teenage boy.

It would have been easier to head toward failure than it would have been for me to find my place in a world that at times made me feel as if there was no way out.

Four years of wasted time in a gang was nothing compared to what laid ahead for me—the rest of my life and what I chose to make of it. The choice would be mine and mine alone. Only the strong survived when the odds were against you.

If I learned anything from my parents, it was that hard work and the will to do better was always the way to go. I only wished I would have remembered that sooner though, but regrets would remain, after all, they're part of life. It was only if I let them rule me would it lead to a life filled with one catastrophe after another. A road I had no desire to continue going down.

So, at sixteen, a gang member since I'd turned twelve, with fuel burning in my blood—I was determined to change my life around. Later, when I looked back, I'd wish I had the revelation sooner, it possibly could have kept my dad from paying the price for my bad choice. Or maybe not.

Every decision, circumstance, and action would define me as a man one day. The question was— what type of man did I want to become?

Destiny: *the events that will necessarily happen to a particular person or thing in the future.*

However, what happens when events occur to two people, and they cross at some point?

I'll tell you the answer.

My life.

Her life.

Our life.

two paths *One* destiny

Chapter One

The gang's turf consisted of a three-block radius. A step past the invisible division line in either direction would place a member inside another gang's territory. It's hard to believe so many gangs exist, but they do. I would know. I'm Luca Lucio Moretti, and for the last four years, my life revolved around them.

As a member, it's guaranteed someone close to you, if not yourself, life would be cut short. With enough time spent in a gang, another guarantee was local jail, or a prison term would be served at some point. I had been lucky I hadn't done a stint in juvie like several of the other younger members already had. And believe me, it wasn't from lack of trying by the local cops, they just never obtained tangible proof that would allow them to drag me in.

The involvement of kids in gangs gets blamed on the circumstances surrounding us. Like the area we live in or our family dynamics. Whether we live in a poverty-stricken area with a high unemployment rate. The educational system even gets tagged in the responsibility for not providing quality education. And those providing the statistics love to blame the kids' ethnicity as the number one cause.

Whether the statistics were right or wrong, I had no clue. Personally, I hadn't associated myself with any of the statistics because I hadn't had shitty parents who hadn't given a crap. Nor had I lived in a poor neighborhood in one of New York City's boroughs. Don't get me wrong, my neighborhood was on the poor side. But it was filled with working-class folks with low income.

I really wished there was a defining moment to pinpoint the reason I became a member, but there wasn't. Unless youth and stupidity qualified as reason enough. I would grow older, and I would look back at this time and consider it a waste like many before me. Or maybe as a learning experience. An expensive one since it cost my dad his life.

When I'd join, I had been nothing but a twelve-year-old who'd thought it would be cool to belong and let the pressure from others around me lead me into making a bad choice.

So here I sat at sixteen beside my mom in the front row as the priest spoke over my dad's ashes. I glanced over my shoulder at the people in attendance. A few family members, friends, neighbors, and even cabbies who worked for the same cab company as my dad. Every person had come to honor my dad and pay their respects to my family.

Even Mr. Sudan, who owned the corner store, had shown up. I'd never be able to repay him for looking the other way when I lifted things from his store. If he'd turned me in, I would have joined the many young boys from my neighborhood with juvie records and became another statistic. Who knows? Maybe I would have benefitted from a stay, or I might have taken a bigger step into criminal activity.

Though I would always wonder what turn my life would have taken if he had turned me in to the cops. There was always the chance I would have wised up sooner.

Looking around, it was funny the ones missing at the memorial service were my supposed gang brothers. The ones who talked about loyalty and watching each other's back and so much other bullshit. Out of all of them, the only member I gave a crap about was my best friend, Davis. We had joined at the same time, and though I knew I wasn't responsible for anyone else's decision, I wondered if it hadn't been for me would he have succumbed to the pressure and joined. As for the rest of them, I hadn't heard anything since my dad had been shot and killed.

That weighed more on me than anything else. The loss of my dad opened my eyes to what/who were important in my life. My dad's death would always be the single most important regret I would carry through my life. And I was sure there would be other regrets. They just wouldn't top the loss of him.

Joseph Luca Moretti had been well liked around our neighborhood, so the turnout for his memorial service shouldn't have shocked me. He worked hard to provide for my mom and me. Even in the times when he'd come home tired from a long day hauling people to where they needed to go, he never turned his back on a neighbor who asked for help.

My dad had taught me many things throughout my sixteen years. He taught me to ride a bike and throw a ball. He had read to me as a small child, and then after I learned to read, he listened. He had shared his love of boxing with me and even saved for months to take me to a fight at Madison Square Gardens. He'd helped with homework and entertained me with stories or games when I was too sick to go to school. But what I would remember most of all was that he loved me unconditionally. Would my own children one day be able to say or feel the same about me?

He and my mom showed me love even in times when I hadn't deserved it. If I closed my eyes, I would be able to see the disappointed look on his face, the one I had seen the day I walked into the room wearing gang colors for the first time or every time I smarted off. There were times he voiced his dislike and disappointment in me, but he never needed to.

18

The morning of the day he died was the last time I would witness his disappointment. I'd walked in the kitchen and grabbed a piece of toast off the table. *"Later," I said as I turned and headed back through the doorway that led to the hallway toward the front door.*

"Hold up there, Lucio. Where are you headed this early?" he questioned from his spot at the table where he sat with his coffee and newspaper as he did every morning.

I stopped and looked over my shoulder. "Out," I replied with the typical tone I perfected as if I was grown and answered to no one.

He slowly folded the paper and set it down on the table before he looked at me. "Your disrespect for me and your mother is less appreciated under my roof as each day goes by. When are you going to wake up and realize that group of hoodlums are not your friends?"

"Do we have to do this now? Davis is waiting." I sighed.

"We love you, Lucio. But it won't be enough to keep you out of prison."

"Christ, I'm not going to prison."

"Maybe not today or tomorrow, but eventually, if you stay on this path of destruction."

It was the same speech I'd heard a hundred times. I blew out a breath and said, "Whatever. Got it. I'm meeting Davis," then I headed for the front door and walked out.

I was a typical kid on the cusp of my teenage

years who thought I knew more than my parents or any adult for that matter. So, every time I let him and my mom down would be another regret added to my list.

The service ended, and my mom slipped her arm in mine, and I helped her stand. Before we had taken two steps, people began approaching us and offering their condolences. I wasn't sure how much time passed before everyone left, leaving only family standing in the room.

I walked with my mom to where my dad's urn sat with framed pictures surrounding it.

"Collect the pictures, Lucio," my mom said as she let go of my arm and reached for the urn.

"Let me get that, Mom." I reached for the ashes, and she waved me off.

"I need to do this," was all she said as she curled her arm around it and lifted it to her.

When we turned, my uncle Tony was walking toward us. "Are you ready, Gina?" he asked as he reached us. Uncle Tony and his family made the trip to New York City from Boston, where they lived and owned a restaurant. He was my mom's older brother.

"Oh, Tony, what am I going to do without Joe?" she asked him and swiped at the few tears that ran down her cheeks.

"Like you have been, honey. One day at a time. Just know you aren't alone. Maria and I are here for you," he said and placed a hand at her elbow.

My mom nodded and let Uncle Tony lead her

20

toward the exit. At the SUV, as he helped her into the passenger side, I slid into the back with my aunt and two cousins. The ride to our house was quiet, and when Uncle Tony stopped the vehicle, I got out with the photos and carried them inside. After I sat them on the table, I headed to my bedroom and shut the door.

I wanted to better my life, so my dad would be proud of me. Not belittle everything he and mom sacrificed so I could have one. But with anything worth having, I'd have to work for it, and the road to a better life would most definitely be rough and filled with several potholes waiting for me to fall in.

However, once I was on that road, everything that happened before to get me there, apart from losing my dad, I'd do ten times over to reach it again. After all, bad choices set me on the path of destruction as my dad had said, so it would be my choices that would lead me further down the same path or allow me to carve a new one.

The first step would be to sever my connection with the gang. And like I mentioned before, it wouldn't come easy or without pain, but I'd take everything dealt to me because my dad was right when he'd say nothing worthwhile comes without a price. I speak of them as past tense because the day my dad died was my last association. Cutting ties wouldn't be easy, but for me, it would be worth it. Life had too much to offer me. I refused to end up as another faceless statistic.

Walking to my bed, I sat, placed my head in my

hands and let the tears flow for my dad.

Chapter Two

"Lucio! Davis is here," my mom yelled, then the door to my bedroom opened, and he walked in.

"What's up with you? I haven't heard anything from you for a couple weeks. You haven't come next door, and the few times I came over here, your mom said you didn't want to see me. You haven't even been to Trace's place to hang out," he said as he plopped down on the bottom of my bed.

I closed the magazine I had been flipping through and looked at my best friend. Davis and I had been friends since the day he and his family had moved into the house next door. From that point on we'd been almost inseparable.

At the age of four, the biggest worry for both of us was if our parents had enough money so we could get an ice cream at the corner store on a hot day. We started school together. We faced bullies together. And we'd broken under the pressures of our neighborhood and joined the local street gang together. It'd been easy to get accepted. Getting out, not so much.

Davis frowned when I hadn't immediately spoken. Because I wasn't sure when I did if it would be the last words between us, so I wanted to prolong what was possibly the last minutes shared with my best friend.

"Yo, you going to talk or what?" he asked. "I came to check on you. Trace and the others have asked about you. Everyone's wondering why you haven't been around."

"Sure, I bet they've been real interested in where I've been. Since none of the crew has shown any concern for me in the past month." I rolled my eyes. Outside of Davis, not one had checked on me.

"What's up with you, Luca?" Davis asked, using my first name. The only ones who called me Lucio were my parents.

I took a deep breath, then let it out. "I'm out. Or I will be," I said and watched my friend's facial expression change as it hit him what I meant.

"You know it's not that easy, Luca. We aren't in a club like the boy scouts where you can just stop going to meetings, and there are no consequences."

"The boy scouts. Seriously," I said and chuckled. It felt good even if it was for a brief moment.

Davis smiled and shook his head. "Hey, you caught me off guard, and it was the only reference I could come up with on the fly. Cut a brother a break."

"Well, I guess it isn't too far off. The scouts do

24

wear colors. It just happens to be a whole uniform, though." I grinned back. I'd missed the easy comradery with my friend.

I'd done nothing for the last few days but sit in my room and think over everything one of the detectives handling my dad's case had told my mom when he called to inform her that they'd made an arrest. Mom had hung up the phone and broke down, but the sobs and tears were different. When she'd composed herself, she started to fill me in on the call.

"Lucio, that was Detective Wilson. He called to let us know they made an arrest in your dad's case. He's positive they have the right person, too. They found a gun on the boy, and they are only waiting to get the...the ballistics back to confirm what they already know."

After she finished giving me all the information, she wiped her cheeks, and for the first time since we lost my dad, she smiled. Not a full-blown smile, but I'd take the partial upward curve of her lips any day over witnessing her daily tears and hearing the soft cries each night from her bedroom.

I shook my head and focused back on my friend as he continued to talk. "The difference between the boy scouts and us is they can quit at any time and don't have to worry about getting beat or worse. You know Trace isn't going to let you just walk away quietly like it's no big deal."

"It's really not up to him," I said and swung my

25

legs off the bed and sat on the edge.

"Fuck, Luca, I know you've been through a bad time with losing your pops and all, but I didn't think it would make you lose your mind," Davis said and ran his hand over his head.

"No, I actually started using it."

"That's nice, but I hope you aren't used to it. 'Cause you won't be able to use your brain for long if Trace decides to put a bullet in it. Which is a good possibility."

"It doesn't matter. Either way, I'm out, Davis. There's no going back for me."

"Luca, you aren't thinking straight. Give it some time before you make that decision. I think your emotions are high and you're not thinking straight."

I stood and looked down at my friend. "No, I'm not going to wait or put it off. For the first time in a while, I've got my eyes wide open, Davis."

"Eyes wide open to what, Luca? You're making no sense."

"The cops caught and arrested the guy who shot my dad."

"Okay, that's good news. But I still don't understand what that has to do with you staying away from Trace's place and talking about breaking ties to the gang," Davis said as he held his hands out palms up and shrugged.

I looked my closest friend in the eyes and said, "It was Louis." I watched the shock cross Davis' face the second the name registered.

"What? Louis. As in Louis, the kiss ass and Trace's lapdog?" I nodded, and he shook his head and continued. "Shit, he hasn't been around for the last week, but no one has mentioned anything about him being arrested. At least not in front of me." Davis ran his hand down his face, then looked back at me. "Come on, it has to be a mistake. The cops got the wrong guy. You know it happens. Besides, they've been after Trace for years even before we joined. Maybe it's a plan to finally bust up the gang."

"Davis, they aren't framing Louis or Trace for that matter. They don't have the wrong guy. When they tracked Louis down, they found the gun that was used in his possession."

"That doesn't mean he did it. They could have planted the gun after the fact. There has to be an explanation for it."

"There is. Louis wanted to move up the ladder, and he did a robbery to get Trace's attention." I shrugged. "Louis has never liked being the low man of the crew. He wanted to be Trace's go-to man."

"Louis is only fifteen. Regardless of what he wanted, he had to know Trace wouldn't move him up the chain and place him in the know. Trace has never included any of the younger members when he and his lieutenants, as he calls them, have sit-downs."

"Evidently, he thought he would be the first." I shook my head. "Trace doesn't worry about us younger guys. We're expendable. He doesn't care if

27

we serve time in juvie or even jail. It's about trust with him. Who he trusts, not if they trust him. Trace doesn't want to serve jail time any more than the next guy. He definitely doesn't want to go down because the cops put pressure on someone, and they flipped on him."

"You don't think Trace singled your dad out, do you?"

"Nah, I don't think that. The detective said it was a robbery gone bad. My dad was handing over the cash he had in the cab. While he was doing it. The old lady he was waiting for walked out of the building. Right in the middle of it. They think it startled Louis, and he reacted by shooting my dad."

"Damn. This whole thing is a fucked-up mess. But come on, Luca, it was an accident. Not as if Trace sent him to do it," Davis said, then stood from the bed.

"I can't answer to what Louis thought or if he even knew my dad. But it doesn't change how I feel. And I feel my association with Louis and the gang makes me just as responsible for what happened. I let my dad down, and he paid the price for my stupidity."

"Luca, you can't believe that. It's not like you knew Louis was going to rob someone and you offered up your dad. That's crazy, man."

"It doesn't matter how it happened, Davis. I've had days to think about it. My dad was disappointed in me for becoming part of Trace's gang. He and my mom expected much better from me, and I let them both down. I can't change what happened to my dad, but I can change what happens to me going forward. And if I'm lucky, maybe my mom can be proud of me again. I've done some crappy things in the last few years, and I can't take them back, but I can damn well change the course I'm on. I just wish I'd been a month sooner with my revelation." I placed a hand on Davis' shoulder. "You've been a great friend, and I don't expect you to follow me in my departure. Like you said, we don't know what Trace will do, and it really doesn't matter to me. I'm out whether he agrees to it or not. You shouldn't have to take on my fight."

"Seriously? Do you think I won't have your back in this? Haven't I always had your back, Lucio? You've been my friend since the first day we met. I've only known the others for four years. I'll always choose you over them."

Davis was and would always be the best friend I had. Him acknowledging that he felt the same about me was more than I deserved. I would forever believe that he wouldn't have gotten tied up with Trace and his crew, if not for me.

"You'll never know how much I appreciate the support. I guess if you're with me, there's no time like the present to face what Trace decides to dish out," I said as I slapped Davis' shoulder.

"Yeah. But hopefully, it's an ass beating and not a bullet to the head. Definitely not feeling that today."

"I think I got something to keep that from happening." I reached for an envelope on my nightstand and handed it to Davis. He raised the unsealed flap and pulled out the folded paper and began to read. When he finished, he gave both the envelope and sheet of paper back to me.

"Shit, that list is of everything Trace had and is involved in for at least as long as we've been with the crew. Some of that stuff we were involved in, too. We could go down with the rest of them if the cops get their hands on the list."

"Not if he lets us walk. On the chance he doesn't—we'll probably be dead. So..." I shrugged my shoulders, then took the envelope and stuffed the paper inside. After I opened the door to my small closet, I reached on the shelf for an old box holding comic books from my younger days. I slipped the envelope between the pages of the one on top. Setting the box back on the shelf, I closed the closet door and turned to face my friend.

"Awesome, but who's going to find it if you hide the information?" Davis asked.

"Use your head. Do you think the cops won't go through everything in our houses if our bodies turn up?"

"True. So... I guess I'm ready if you are," Davis said, then sighed.

I walked to my bedroom door with Davis following me. "Let's get this done, and then we will come back, nurse our wounds and celebrate," I said as I pulled the door open.

"The first thing we toast to is to being able to breathe," Davis said in a lower voice to probably keep my mom from overhearing.

"A little obsessed with death, man?" I asked as we walked toward the front door.

"Only when it is a good possibility," Davis answered.

As we passed the living room, I told my mom I was going out and the only response I received was the look of sadness that crossed her face before she turned her head away.

Davis and I walked out the door, and as we headed in the direction of Trace's place, my thoughts went to how damaged the relationship with my parents really was. I hoped after everything was said and done, I'd have time to repair it. At least where my mom was concerned.

two paths *O*ne destiny

Chapter Three

Heads turned in mine and Davis' direction as we approached Trace's house. On the small porch, some of the guys sat. While the others either sat on the steps or in the yard.

"Yo, look who decided to grace us with his presence," Trace said from the doorway as we reached the sidewalk in front of his house.

"Ya know, been a little busy with my dad's death and all," I said and stepped into the yard.

Trace raised his hand and rubbed his cheeks and chin between his thumb and fingers before answering me. "Yeah, I was sorry to hear about that. Shouldn't have kept you from checking in with me, though."

Standing there, looking around at the others and listening to Trace, I wondered how I ever thought belonging would be cool. Everyone, other than Trace's lieutenants, were nothing but expendable bodies. The ones who ran his errands, delivered and sold his drugs, or even committed petty thefts to amuse him and prove their loyalty.

To include me. In return, we received a little pocket change for our troubles.

"Thanks. As for me checking in with you, I'd think that would go both ways. Since we're supposed to have each other's backs and all."

Trace's eyes narrowed at my tone. "Yeah, didn't think your family would appreciate us there. Besides, Davis represented," he said with a chin lift in Davis' direction.

"Huh, I think it had more to do with Louis being responsible for my dad's death than you worried if my family accepted you." At my words, a few of the guys stood and moved closer to Trace.

Trace's entire facial expression turned cold and mean. The look at one time would've had me taking a step back or apologizing for having stepped out of line. But not anymore. Once I walked away today, I would spend every minute of my future trying to atone for my poor judgment.

"You forget who you're talking to, boy?"

"Nope. I know. It's just I don't care anymore. I'm out," I said, and other than several snickers, no one said a word.

Trace glanced around, then chuckled when his eyes came back to me. "You think it's that easy. You come to my house, then start telling me how things are going to work," he said to me, then shifted his eyes to Davis. "Don't hear anything coming out of your mouth, Davis. You letting your boy speak for you now?"

Even though Davis stood beside me, no way

would I take my eyes off Trace and the others to look in his direction.

After a brief pause, Davis answered, "I'm with Luca."

"Ah, the little friends who joined together want to leave together. What makes either of you think I'd just let you walk? Nothing in life is easy or free. There are dues to pay."

"You're right," I agreed, and a smug look surfaced on Trace's face, but as quickly as it formed, it was washed away when I continued. "But paying dues goes for everyone. I guess it comes down to what price you are willing to pay. There's a list of everything you've done or thought of doing, time and dates included, waiting to be turned over to the cops. I figure since arresting Louis; they got a hard-on waiting for one break in the case to tie him to you along with my dad's robbery and death. Plus, anything else they can tack on would be gravy for them."

"You don't know shit about anything. I had nothing to do with that dumbass shooting your dad."

"Maybe you did, maybe you didn't. What matters is it is written down. Do ya think the cops are going to care what you have to say? They will take the information and run with it, then investigate the information after they have you and the other locked up. You might be willing take the chance I'm lying to you, but how many of your *boys* are willing to that chance."

"You don't have the balls...boy, and honestly, I don't give a shit." I could tell by his facial expression that what he said and what he was thinking were two different things. He just didn't want to show weakness in front of the others. I couldn't have my life spiraling any longer. No matter what the outcome of today was.

"Your call, man. Whatever you decide, the ending will be the same. Davis and I will be out one way or another. The difference is that if we walk, you get to go on for another day. If we don't, then it will give the cops even more charges to add to the ones your long list of illegal activities brings." There was silence as Trace, and I were in a stare down. When his expression changed, I knew he had come to a decision. Not a good one as far as Davis and I were concerned.

"I'm tired of dealing with you," Trace said, then waved his hand out in our direction. The movement had the others jumping up and lunging at Davis and me.

Punches were thrown, and kicks were landed. I felt each one as they connected with my body. Even with Davis and I fighting back, we were outnumbered. I knew this beating would be worse than the beating I'd endured to become a part of Trace's crew.

The blow to the back of my head had instant pain radiating through my skull, then the darkness started to consume me. I glanced in Davis' direction and saw him take a punch to the face as the sound of sirens rend the air. The last thing I heard as I lost consciousness was the squealing tires followed by gunfire.

I struggled with the darkness and fought the feeling of being lost. The effort used to push forward left me exhausted, and no sooner than a speck of light came into view, the darkness pulled me back under.

The next thing I saw was my dad as he smiled and handed me a drink before he sat down beside me. I knew it was a memory surfacing because I had been ten when he'd taken me to the Garden to attend a boxing match.

"This should be a good match. Both men are equally built and within a couple of pounds of each other. Their skill levels are about the same, too. Do you think the champ is going to be able to hold onto the title, Lucio?"

"No. I like the challenger. He's quick with his delivery, and he's a southpaw."

My dad patted my leg. "Just like you, huh?"

"Yeah, but I'm going to be better. I want to be an MMA champ. Do you think I can start taking martial art lessons?" I asked, then took a drink of my soda.

"I thought you wanted to be a boxer."

"Uh huh, until I watched an MMA match on television with Davis and his dad. You get to use

37

more skills, and you get to throw your opponent to the mat."

My dad shook his head. "Yes, and you get much bloodier in MMA than in boxing."

"I know it's freaking awesome." My dad chuckled at the excitement in my voice.

"I'm sure you will be good at whatever you choose to do in life, Lucio," he said and smiled down at me.

The softest of music reached my ears, and I turned my head to see where it was coming from. Instead of the ring and fans in the arena in front of me, there was darkness. I blinked, then glanced back to where my dad and my ten-year-old self was seated only to notice I now stood on the sidewalk in front of my house and though still dark, light filtered into the area from the streetlights.

I scrunched my eyebrows together, not understanding what was going on around me. Through the partially closed curtains on the window, I saw my mom with her face buried in her hands. The scene was unfamiliar to me as far as memories went. It left me struggling with what was happening to me.

A hand landed on my shoulder and squeezed, and I cut my eyes to the side to find my dad standing beside me.

"Dad?" I asked, confused.

"It's time to go back, Lucio."

My dad smiled at me as I stared at him. I

noticed the gray at his temples, which hadn't been there a few minutes ago when we sat in the arena.

This had to be the craziest dream I've ever had.

"Go back? To where? What's going on? We were at the arena waiting for the boxing match to start," I said, then once again glanced around and took in my surroundings.

The only thing I'd ever taken part in was smoking a little weed. And even high, nothing weird happened to me. Maybe I'd gotten ahold of some laced shit. I was going to kick someone's ass if I had. As I debated with myself, music began playing in the background. Besides my breathing, it was the only other sound. A strumming of some sort of stringed instrument, I deduced. I concentrated and tried to guess what type, but instead of figuring it out, I found myself relaxing. It touched something inside me, and I worked to focus on what was real and not what my weird dream state was showing.

Ignoring my dad, I squeezed my eyes shut and let whatever song was being played fill my head.

"Please wake up, Lucio. I can't lose you, too." My mother's voice interrupted the state I was in. I opened my eyes and looked back toward the window, but she was no longer there. Only empty darkness was where my house had previously been. I remembered my dad and glanced around just in time to see the shadow of him in the distance.

"Dad!" I yelled, and he stopped and looked over his shoulder at me. I had figured out he was part of my dream and not real. How could he be? He was dead. As far as I knew, maybe I was, too. Even with that knowledge it was hard to let him go again.

"You're only responsible for your actions in life. Not others' decisions. Make good choices, Lucio, and everything will be okay."

His image started to fade, and I lifted my arm and reached out as if I could grab him and stop him from disappearing. "Dad, wait!"

"I love you, son. I always only be a thought away. Now open your eyes, your mother's waiting." As soon as my dad's words reached my ears, he was gone, and I was left alone in the darkness with music playing in the distance.

I wasn't sure how much time passed as I stood in that spot and continued to listen. I just know when the music ended, a huge weight lifted off me. I no longer felt as though the darkness was swallowing me.

With a sudden burst of strength, I shoved my way through the darkness.

Chapter Four

"Oh my God, Tony, his eyes are open!" I heard my mother yell and squinted my eyes against the brightness blinding me.

"Thank God." I recognized my uncle's voice, though I had no clue as to where he was in the room.

"Lucio? Talk to me, honey," my mom spoke as I fought to bring her into focus.

I opened my mouth with the intention of answering her, but before I could get force any words out, she moved out of my view, and a nurse entered my sightline. At least she was dressed like a nurse. Which meant I was in a hospital unless it was another weird portion of a dream state.

"Welcome back. I'm going to ask you a few questions. Take your time and try to answer them." The nurse voice was soft and as I listened to her, everything that had happened flooded through my mind, bringing along the pain it previously had protected me from.

My mom and uncle stood by while I answered

simple questions like my name and age. My vitals were taken, and then I was poked and prodded by the doctor who entered my room during the nurse's initial evaluation.

After he introduced himself as Dr. Michaels, he informed me that I'd been in a coma for a week and a half. The coma was caused by swelling in my brain from the blow to the back of my head. I had multiple bruises on various parts of my body along with three cracked ribs and a gunshot wound in my shoulder. It had required surgery to remove the bullet.

"You were a lucky young man. The bullet barely grazed the bone before it became lodged. There wasn't a chip, or one fragment of bone found during surgery."

I wanted to tell the doctor I felt anything but lucky.

The doctor talked about recovery time and how long I would be in the hospital. I glanced over to my mom and uncle and noticed tears running down my mom's face. I realized she probably already heard everything that had happened to me, and I hated she had to hear it again.

The most shocking words out of everything the doctor said was I'd been transported from the borough hospital once they'd stabilized me. I was currently in a trauma hospital in the city that specialized in pediatric trauma.

"Pediatric? I'm sixteen, not a baby," I said, feeling more than a little put out being referred to as a kid.

The doctor's lips twitched at my put-out tone. "Pediatric covers from birth to usually sixteen. However, even though you are over our cut off by a few months, we decided you would benefit more from the treatment here."

I felt my eyelids start to droop and fought against it. The last thing I wanted was to go back into the darkness.

"You're going to sleep on and off for the next couple of days. Your system has been stressed from the injuries and surgery. Not to mention the swelling in your head. Though the fluid that kept you in the coma is almost non-existent now, your brain and body still have healing to do. I'll check back in with you later. Rest." Dr. Michaels said. He must have noticed my struggle to stay awake.

I nodded, and Dr. Michaels and the nurse walked out.

As I blinked and started to give in to the heaviness of my eyelids, my uncle moved the chair beside my bed closer for my mom to sit. When she sat and rested a hand on my arm, I rolled my head in her direction. There was one thing I needed to know before I succumbed to the darkness.

"What about Davis? Is he okay?" I asked as my eyes slid closed.

"Sleep, son. We can talk about Davis and everything else when you wake."

I wanted to know about my friend. There was no way I could go under without knowing. "Mom, please. I need to know about Davis."

There was a long pause, and through it I battled to stay in the now. Finally, my mom spoke and the words she said followed me into the darkness.

"I'm so sorry, honey. Davis didn't make it."

A month after being released from the hospital, I found myself in the backseat of my uncle's vehicle and watched the neighborhood I'd grown up in pass by through the window.

I was healed, except for my ribs, which would be tender for a while. And if I stayed away from quick movements, my ribs wouldn't be a problem. They would heal in time. I had no other issues or underlying problems that popped from being in a coma for over a week. However, the verdict was still out on whether I considered it a blessing or not to be on the mend.

Remembering everything from the loss of my dad to the loss of my best friend was the hardest for me to accept. It left me wondering why I was allowed a pass on dying, but Davis wasn't. He'd been my best friend and an even better person. What bothered me the most was I hadn't gotten to say goodbye to my friend or my dad. And no matter what anyone said, even the cops, the weight of responsibility for both deaths pressed down on my shoulders. If I had made better choices—things would be different. There had been so much out of my control.

Over time maybe the weight would lighten. Then again, did it matter? The end result would be the same.

Hell, I'd not only received a pass on death, but was also given a life pass by the cops. They'd came to the hospital and questioned me about the crew, Travis, and why I had been there that day. My story matched with a few people in the neighborhood who'd witnessed what had taken place before the cops had arrived at Travis' place—if it hadn't have been for ones who called the cops and their accounts of what happened matching mine, I'd be in jail, instead of on my way to live in Boston.

It seemed after I went down from the blow to my head, the gunfire hadn't ceased when the police showed up. It continued until everyone in Travis' crew was dead, except for me and Lucas. Lucas had already been in jail and would be going to prison for my dad's death. For me, being the lone survivor paid off. The cops settled for the wipeout of the crew as a win. The part I hated about it, was my friend, Davis, being written off as collateral damage. He'd died in the crossfire when Travis and the others opened fire on the police when they'd arrived on the scene.

Did they honestly think they had a chance? Or was it yet another bad choice that they'd chosen death over jail time.

"You okay back there, Lucio?" my uncle asked with a quick glance over his shoulder and pulled me from my thoughts.

"Yeah, Uncle Tony, I'm good," I answered, then leaned my head back and rested it against the headrest.

"It'll be nice having my sister and nephew around," my uncle said.

My mom chuckled. "We'll see if you say that after we've been at your house for a while, Tony."

"Gina, you're always welcome at my house. And you can stay as long as you need to. It's what family does for one another. Maria is so excited to have you both at the house. She's been busy fixing up your rooms. She's even notified the high school about Lucio's enrollment. They'll have the paperwork ready when you go in to register him. School will be starting in a few weeks."

I closed my eyes as if that would keep me from thinking about starting at a new school. I kept them closed and listened to my mom and uncle talk. My uncle mentioned again how the move was a good idea since we had nothing holding us in New York. That leaving behind the bad memories and having a fresh start was exactly what we needed.

I began to doze, and my last thought was, *I hope he is right.*

two paths *O*ne destiny

Chapter Five

Pulling the zipper around the sides on my suitcase, I closed it, then lifted it off the bed and placed it on the floor next to my violin case. With everything ready for my trip, I walked out of my room.

"Did you finish packing?" my mom asked as I entered the kitchen.

"Yes, but I still don't understand why we have to leave a day early to go shopping. The first scheduled rehearsal isn't until late afternoon the next day. Why not get there early that morning, and we can shop before or after the rehearsal?"

"I thought it would be nice for us to have some girl time. We've not done it in a long time. Besides, you need an outfit for the performance," my mom said, then sighed. "You're the one who refused to let me buy something here without you present. I even volunteered to bring them home for your approval."

I opened the refrigerator and grabbed a bottle of water before replying. The battle over clothing had been an ongoing affair between my mother and me since…well, forever.

Constance Chambers, my mother, believed appearance meant everything. Even while cooking dinner the woman wore black linen slacks and an off-white blouse. On her neck was a strand of pearls with matching earrings on her lobes. There wasn't one blonde hair on her head out of place, and if I looked down at her feet, I knew I would find her standard two-inch heeled shoes. What she considered the acceptable 'in the house' footwear for daytime.

I looked down at what I had on: yoga pants, an oversized t-shirt with my high school's mascot and name on the front, and no shoes on my feet. When it came to clothes, my opinion never came close to my mom's. It wasn't as if I didn't know when to dress appropriately, it was just she and I had different ideas in what classified as appropriate.

"Because you would have brought home what you like, instead of what I like," I said as I plucked a slice of cucumber from the salad bowl.

"Stop that. Your father will be home any minute, and we'll eat," Mom said as she swatted my hand away when I went in for another slice. "There's nothing wrong with my taste in clothing. You just like to be difficult. It would be nice to see you wear something besides black slacks. Maybe a nice skirt for a change."

"I'm not wearing a floor length skirt, ever. Skirts are annoying. Pants are comfortable, and I don't have to worry if I'm going to get my foot tangled in the hem when I stand from my seat. People are supposed to be there to enjoy the music, not to inspect our clothing."

"Sometimes, I wonder how you can be my daughter," my mom mumbled.

It was something she frequently said when we had a difference in opinions. She never said it to be mean. It was more of a teasing statement. Our likes and dislikes differed for most everything. Heck, we only shared one, no two physical attributes: our body frames were both on the thin side with the slightest of curves, and I had inherited her pale skin. Where she was considered tall at five feet nine with blonde hair and blue eyes. I was average at five feet six with brown hair and brown eyes.

I was my father's daughter when it came to looks. I just wished I'd gotten his skin tone because instead of tanning, I turned into one big freckle. I would have liked a smidgeon more in height, too. Though I was told my height was from the women on my father's side, who were average in height, while the men ranged in height by inches, and all were over six feet. In my dad's case, he topped off at six feet four.

"You should know how I became your daughter. One night approximately sixteen years ago, I'm guessing in the bedroom, when you and Dad— " I cut off what I was going to say and started laughing when she gently shoved me on the shoulder.

51

"Olivia!" The tone of her voice as she said my name along with the shocked looked on her face, only made me laugh harder.

"What are my favorite two girls up to?" I stopped laughing and smiled at my dad.

"Well, it seems Mom has a little confusion with me being her daughter. I was trying to tell her, but she didn't want to hear any of it."

"Because you're fifteen and I'm your mother. Plus, ladies don't talk like that."

"You should have at least corrected her, Constance. She's wrong," my dad said as he leaned in and kissed my mom on the cheek.

"Wrong about what?" I asked as I opened the cabinet and reached to grab the dinner plates.

"On the where, and it wasn't at night. It was daylight, sometime in the afternoon to be exact, and happened in the living room. I distinctly remember the day. I'd been out of town for a couple of days on a case, and when I walked in the door, your mother jumped me. It was hours later before we made it upstairs to the bedroom."

"Richard, I did no such thing!" My mom scolded while I giggled.

"You did, and if you play your cards right, Constance, I'll let you jump me later in our bedroom."

"Good Lord, Richard, go change while Olivia and I set the table for dinner. You say the most outrageous things."

Most teenagers would be doing the finger in

the mouth with gagging sounds if their parents said such things in front of them. We liked to think our parents didn't have sex. I personally thought it was stupid, but then again, my parents had no problem showing they loved each other. I witnessed it every day, from the way they looked at each other, spoke to each other. The smallest of touches as they passed each other entering or exiting a room. They still held hands when they were out. Not once had I felt embarrassed with their acts of affection. Instead, observing them made me want the same type of relationship one day.

"Yes, sweetheart. We wouldn't want Olivia to know you are unable to keep your hands off me," my dad said and turned to head out of the room.

I smiled as my mom shook her head, then spoke loud enough for my dad to hear as he walked down the hallway toward the stairs.

"Choose your husband wisely, Olivia. Bad boys may be exciting at the time, but as you grow older, trust me, they tend to test your last nerve."

My dad laughed, then yelled back, "Please, you would have been bored in six months if you'd married the type of man your mother wanted for you. Lucky for you that you were smart enough to choose me. You haven't regretted a day in seventeen years." I heard his shoes on the stairs as he headed to the second floor.

I may have chuckled at his teasing. But the fact I couldn't picture my dad as a bad boy didn't mean others didn't see him that way. I mean, I wasn't

53

deaf; I'd heard whispered remarks by some of the other moms over the years. Especially when he wore short-sleeved pullover shirts revealing the tattoos down his arms. And that was only his arms. My dad had tattoos covering his chest and back, too, from the time he spent in the Navy.

"I swear I don't know how he stands upright with that swollen head. His shoulders have to ache from carrying it around," she said.

"Maybe he's allergic to the ink in the tattoos. Over the years it could be causing his head to swell," I said and tried to hold a straight face as my mom stared at me. I couldn't hold back and busted out laughing. At first my mom just stared at me, then she threw her head back and laughed.

I'd forgotten how much fun it was to hang out with my mom. Probably because my days had been full for the last two years. I was either tied up with a school function or attending practices for the BYSO (Boston Youth Symphony Orchestras), where I was a violinist.

Maybe spending the day shopping with my mom wouldn't be so bad. I did used to love girl time as she called it.

Chapter Six

The closer we got to New York, the heavier the traffic became. We hadn't gotten on the road as early as my mom had wanted, and the delay placed us in the middle of lunchtime traffic. Not that traffic in and around New York City was ever mild. Well, maybe in the early hours like three in the morning.

We were staying at the Whitby in Manhattan, and when we reached the area, the traffic was less congested, if only a little.

"How far to the hotel?" I asked as we stopped at yet another red light.

"Not much longer. A few more blocks. Once we get there and check in, how about we walk or cab our way around?" Mom asked as a driver blew their car horn and then maneuvered around a vehicle in the middle of the intersection in front of us.

"I'm glad Boston isn't quite this bad. But I guess that's why a lot of people don't get their licenses here."

"Boston might not be as heavy in traffic, but we do have more young people on the road than New York City does."

"I'll be one of those young drivers soon. Well, after I go through the driver's education course. I'm not sure when I'll find the time to take it, though. Just think, once I pass, you won't have to haul me around all the time."

"You've got months until you turn sixteen, Olivia. There's time to figure it out," Mom said as the light turned green and she accelerated.

"I know, but—" The sound of squealing tires stopped me mid-sentence and had my eyes glancing out my mom's driver side window only to see the front end of a huge truck. The next thing I felt was the impact as the truck, which must have missed the light change, crashed into our vehicle.

The force buckled the car and glass broke as the metal bent. Airbags exploded, and mine slammed me back against my seat. I heard a scream and realized it came from me. Everything happened so fast, and when it was over, the airbags deflated, I raised my hand to my head and felt moisture. I hadn't even remembered hitting my head, but I must have hit the side window during the accident.

I heard people yelling and looked around and saw movement outside the car, then I turned my head to check on my mom and froze. The sight of her condition was too much. Blood ran down her face, her head was at an odd angle, her body turned toward me, and the seat twisted in its frame. I reached for her hand closest to me and grabbed hold, then I leaned my head back against my seat. I must have closed my eyes at one point because I no longer saw any light. I looked into darkness.

Who knew it only took a few seconds to change your life?

Sirens could be heard, the sound growing louder as they neared. Other than that, I was left with the sound of my own breathing, closing out everything else around me. I don't know how long I sat there holding my mom's hand. Time seemed to stand still.

Afraid to move, I waited. I'd never felt so alone. I was jarred by the sound of doors opening and footsteps on the pavement that grew louder as they got closer. Voices began to surround me.

"Passenger is awake. Looks to be in shock." I guessed the man must've been talking about me as the wind hit me when my door was opened.

"Not getting a pulse here. We're going to need the truck moved more out of the way, so we can get in here and work. It's going to take the jaws to get this side open." Another man's voice joined the mix as I listened to everything happening around me.

I wanted to yell and tell them to help my mom. I wanted to ask if they thought she would be alright. I wanted to know what was happening around us. But I knew the answers. I would never forget anything about the moment—it was when my life changed.

"Let's get a neck brace on her and get her out of the vehicle," was said by someone, then I heard the rustling of clothing all around me before hands touched my neck.

"Just going to put this brace on your neck and give you something to take the edge off while we move you. You'll still have a little discomfort, but it shouldn't be too bad."

I felt a prick in my leg, then my head was lifted off the rest only enough for the brace to be wrapped around and fastened.

"Ready to pull her out," came from the one beside me. Then I felt a hand touch mine. The one holding my mom's hand. "If you have to let go of her, honey, so we can get you out."

As soon as I loosened my grip, my arm and hand were brought to my side. I felt the loss instantly as the final connection to my mom was broken.

Hands grabbed me, and I was lifted out of the car, then lowered. I felt pressure on different points of my body.

"We're strapping you in for travel. Can you tell us your name, sweetie?" a woman's voice asked.

I wasn't sure if I could speak, but I nodded my head and focused on the question. I struggled to push the one word out. "Olivia," my voice strained and barely over a whisper.

"Hang in there. We're going to take care of

you, Livi. We're going to get you to the hospital as fast as we can," the woman said, using the shortened version of my name.

I didn't respond, there was no need. My nose and mouth were covered with a mask, and then I was moving. Things seemed to move in slow motion, yet I had a feeling that was more me and due to whatever they'd given me in the shot.

The sounds around me began to blend, and the voices jumbled to where not one stood out above the others, leaving me to fade into myself.

The next clear voices I heard were when I laid on a bed with beeping sounds in the background. The hospital just as the woman said.

I struggled to remember the ride to the hospital. How long had it been?

"Are you Olivia's doctor?"

Dad? I heard my dad's voice, but I couldn't tell where it was coming from. He wasn't with us in the car. He wasn't even with us in New York. How did he get here so quickly?

"Yes, Mr. Chambers. I'm Dr. Michaels, and I was hoping to speak with you before you go in to see your daughter?" My dad must have nodded instead of answering because the doctor continued. "She has several deep lacerations that have been stitched. Several areas of bruising on her torso and some on her face. She was in and out of consciousness in the ambulance while they were in route. When she arrived in the ER, we thought it best to keep her sedated until we could evaluate

59

any damage and keep her stabilized. Once we were sure we'd treated everything, we cut back on the meds, and brought her out from under the drugs. She has a—"

"My wife? I wasn't given any information when I was notified other than Constance and Olivia had been in an accident and brought here. Is my wife here, too or not?" My dad asked after cutting the doctor off.

I laid listening to my dad and the doctor. They had to be standing a little way down the hall because I had to strain to hear them.

"I'm sorry for your loss, Mr. Chambers. Your wife was brought into the ER, but... They worked on her at the scene. However, they were unable to get a heartbeat. Mrs. Chambers was already gone at the scene."

There was a quiet moment, and I lifted my arm, the one that had nothing attached to it, and wiped the tears away with my hand. Tears that were making steady tracks down my cheeks after it was verified that my mom was really dead. I'd hoped when I'd woken that I'd been wrong with what had happened. That maybe I had just been disoriented at the scene of the accident.

I wasn't sure how many minutes passed before I heard my dad's voice again and he asked, "Were you in the ER when they brought them in?"

"Yes, I was called down for Olivia. I work in pediatrics, Mr. Chambers."

"Livi?" my dad's voice roughened and was

lower than when he'd spoken before. So low, I was barely able to make out what he said.

"We'll go into Olivia's room shortly. I'd like to finish discussing privately on her condition."

"On her condition? What do you mean? What's wrong? Is she going to be alright, Dr. Michaels?"

"On top of everything I stated before, she has a mild concussion. Her right forearm is broken and is bandaged as of right now. A cast will be put on as soon as the swelling subsides. Aside from that, our concern is..." the doctor's voice lowered, and I couldn't hear his voice or even my dad's anymore. The only sounds I was picking up around me were the machines in my room.

I laid in the bed and tried to recall what had happened after I'd regained consciousness. The more I tried to focus, the pounding in my head was brought front and center, which caused me to moan from the piercing pain. In one of my lucid moments in the ambulance, I remembered they touched the side of my head, and I'd flinched. The area had been tender.

Then I remembered I had touched my head in the car after the accident and there'd been blood been blood. I had to have hit the window when the airbag exploded. Everything was still so foggy and the harder I tried to remember, the more my head hurt.

"I will be back in a few hours to check on Olivia again. Mr. Chambers, she really will be fine after a

61

little recovery time. And again, I'm sorry for the loss of your wife. I wish there were more that could have been done." The doctor's voice was louder and seemed as if he was closer to my room.

"Thank you, Dr. Michaels," my dad said, and I heard footsteps walking away, then a whoosh of the door being pushed open. I looked toward the direction of the sound.

"Oh, Livi, sweetheart," my dad said, and tears ran down my cheeks as I began to cry. "It's going to be alright, baby." He gently held on to me and rubbed my back. The hug quite awkward due to my wrapped arm that was secured across my middle. With my face buried in his shoulder, I sobbed until there was nothing left in me. I turned my face and rested my cheek against him and let him continue to hold me.

"Dad, I can't see," I whispered, acknowledging for the first time that I'd lost my sight.

"I know. We'll get through this together, Livi. I promise," he said, and I nodded while soaking up the warmth of being in his arms offered.

Chapter Seven

Several days later and after what seemed like a hundred test administered for my sudden blindness, I was finally going to be released to go home. My diagnosis was 'conversion disorder/hysteria', which the doctors said was brought on by the traumatic experience. It could last days, weeks, even months. It would be totally up to me and how I processed what happened. As if it was my choice to live in darkness. Therapy was discussed to help pull me through. I'd even had a visit from a pediatric psychologist.

That had been fun. Not! How was I supposed to feel—I'd lost my mom. She died beside me. I don't know who wouldn't consider that traumatic.

My dad had been busy between staying with me at the hospital and having to handle everything dealing with the accident. To include making the arrangements for my mom's body to be transferred to Boston. Then after we got home, the planned funeral.

"Hey, kiddo. How are you feeling today?" my

dad asked as he pushed through the door and entered my room.

I forced a smile. One I wasn't feeling because I knew he was trying to stay upbeat for me while trying to deal with his own grief. I lost my mom, and he lost the love of his life.

How did families get through this?

"Okay, I guess. This cast is a pain, though. I kept hitting myself with it in my sleep."

"It's only for six weeks. At least it is only to your elbow. And your fingers are free."

"Ugh, I'll still have it when school starts. That will be loads of fun. Well... unless my sight miraculously comes back that is. If it doesn't, then I guess I won't have to worry," I whined.

"Livi, you heard Dr. Michaels. It will come back. There is nothing medically stopping it from doing so. Just relax and be patient. You have some healing to do first."

I blew out a breath. "I know, but Dad, what if they're wrong, and it doesn't come back?" I asked, voicing what was floating around in my head.

"One day at a time, Livi. It's how we'll get through everything. And the first step to moving on starts tomorrow. We'll get you checked out of here and home. Now, I brought something for you." I inhaled deeply, and my dad chuckled. "It isn't food."

"Aww, come on. The food here is horrible, Dad. I'll never take tacos, hamburgers, or pizza for granted again. Well, if it's not anything edible, whatcha bring me?"

There was pause before he said, "Your violin."

"What?" I asked, but it wasn't as if I didn't understand. He'd went and picked up mine and my mom's things that had been in the vehicle.

"I thought maybe you would want to check it over for damages."

I folded my legs up to give him room to lay the case at the foot of my hospital bed. With my free hand, I popped the latches, then opened the lid. I touched the instrument, running my fingers over it. I didn't need my sight to tell if there was physical damage to it. The violin was and had been a part of my life since I began lessons at six years old. Not this particular one of course. It was the one my mom and dad had gifted me with when I'd been accepted into the BYSO just three years ago. I'd been thrilled, it was my favorite color, purple. I might have even more excited over the violin than the actual acceptance into BYSO.

"How about a private concert?" When I didn't immediately answer, my dad continued. "I thought since you missed the performance, you could put one on for me."

The performance. How could I have forgotten about it. It was the reason we came to New York in the first place. I'd been selected to take part in a special orchestra performance that was to include the best from ten different youth orchestras. I was one of four chosen just from our string section. The concert was to be the first of its kind—a youth orchestra made up of some the most talented youth—two long rehearsals—then one night at the Merkin Concert Hall to showcase why we'd been selected as the best. I had worked hard and practice endlessly for hours to learn the violin.

I was six when I begged for a violin and lessons after seeing a violinist on the television playing solo. It had been a documentary my mom was watching, and I'd stopped playing when the woman began her solo. I might not remember her name or the show, but if I concentrated, I could still hear every note she'd played. It had sounded so beautiful.

After my parents bought my first violin and signed me up for lessons—I fell in love playing the violin. But wasn't my love and talent for the instrument that cost me my mom? She and I wouldn't have been at the intersection at that time if not.

"Livi, do you need me to help you lift it out of the case?"

"I'm not sure I can," I whispered. My response having nothing to do with his question.

"If you're worried that holding it will cause pain in your arm, I can help hold it in place. It will be awkward at first, but knowing how much you love to play, I'm sure we can figure out a way to make it work."

I knew my dad was trying to be helpful, but holding my violin wasn't what was on my mind.

"I'm not worried about lifting it or even being

able to play it. If not for me, Mom and I wouldn't have come to here, and she would still be alive," I confessed in a voice barely above a whisper.

"Oh, Livi, no. You are not to blame for what happened. The accident could have just as easily happened in Boston. We don't know why things happen. They just do, sweetheart."

"Are you saying it was like fate? Then fate is cruel."

"I'm not saying that. But your mom believed everyone's life was set from the time they were born," he said, then his hand came down on my shoulder and he squeezed.

I thought about what he said. My mom did believe everything happened for a reason. She's even told me fate was how her and my dad had met. *"Olivia, if I hadn't received a call from the admittance office about missing information on my paperwork when I was in college. I wouldn't have been in the office that day your dad walked in. Fate put us there at the exact time."* I smiled thinking about what she said.

"Help me get it out of the case, please."

My dad was right, it was awkward, but with a little adjustment on my part, I had gotten the violin in place. There was some discomfort using my hand and fingers to hold the end and work the strings with the cast. It was unbearable, though.

With the bow poised, I said, "I hope they don't get mad about me playing and disturbing other patients." Then my fingers worked the strings, and

I slid the bow across. It wasn't as effortlessly as I was used to, and the pain I felt in my arm was less of a distraction with each note. The song I played was one we were to play at the special performance. I guess they still did play it, just without me.

"I See the Light," composed by Alan Menken and lyricist Glenn Slater was written for the Disney animation *Tangled*. Mandy Moore and Zachery Levi were the ones who originally recorded it for their film roles, Rapunzel, and Flynn Rider.

As I visualized the note, I let the music take hold, and as always, everything disappeared around me. All I could hear was the music. All I felt was the violin. The song was about chasing a daydream, living years in a blur until the fog lifts, and at last, I See the Light.

How fitting? I prayed I'd see the light again, too.

When I finished, someone clapped. At first, I thought it was my dad until my doctor spoke, "Wow, Olivia, that was beautiful. You are an exceptionally talented young lady."

"Thank you, Dr. Michaels," I said as I laid the bow down on the bed, then lowered the violin to my lap.

"I hope you didn't receive too many complaints," my dad said. "I just thought it might be good for her to play."

"I don't think so. Who would complain about hearing that? If anything, you may have some of the nurses wanting an encore. I wasn't being polite; you truly are gifted." I felt the heat rise on my face and knew I blushed at the doctor's praise.

"Were you coming to examine Livi, Dr. Michaels?"

"Oh no, I was down at the nurses' station looking over a few charts. When I heard the music, I walked to the doorway so I could get the full effect. I don't get to the symphony often. This was a nice treat."

"Excuse me, Dr. Michaels. You're needed. Your patient is waking up," was said, I assumed by a nurse, interrupting before I could thank the doctor again.

"Fantastic, I'll be right there. Olivia, Mr. Chambers, I will see you both tomorrow morning before I sign the release papers. This is turning out to be a great day."

"See you tomorrow, Dr. Michaels," my dad replied, then I heard the door click closed with Dr. Michaels' departure. "So, what's on the menu for lunch today?"

"Uhh."

Dad chuckled. "Okay. How about I go out and find a pizza joint? If I bring a few pies back for the nurses, too, maybe there won't be any complaints."

"Seriously?"

"Anything for you, sweetheart. I can't let you starve." He kissed me on the cheek, then helped put the violin away. "You rest, and I'll be back before you know it."

After he left, I laid back and closed my eyes. I couldn't blame myself for what happened. Even though, I knew my dad was right, I still felt a tad responsible. There would be rough patches ahead as he and I adjusted to it being only the two of us. I also knew as my dad did—we'd get through it together.

Chapter Eight

Sitting in the family room listening to the television, I smiled when the clanging began in the kitchen. It was close to dinnertime, and the sounds were more than familiar to me after five weeks.

"Livi!"

"Yes, Dad!" I yelled back and tried not to laugh as I did.

"Get changed, we're going out to eat. I'm sick of delivery, and I can't stomach another night of my own cooking."

I rose from the couch and made my way to the kitchen. Since I was still experiencing temporary blindness, I was thankful the layout of our home never changed.

"Dad, are you okay?" I asked when I reached the kitchen and heard him shuffling around. He was probably putting everything back he'd initially pulled out to fix for dinner.

"Fuck, your mother made this shit look so easy. The house was always picked up and clean. She put meals on the table effortlessly. And

71

sonofabitch, how did the woman keep up with the laundry? It's only us. Two people and there is always a new pile of dirty clothes before I'm finished with the previous piles. It's like they multiply when no one's looking."

"Cut yourself a break, Dad. The house was Mom's domain. The woman got excited about cleaning, and she loved to cook. Plus, I helped when I was home. I know you think I'm helpless because I can't see, not to mention the cast, but there are things I could help with that can be done by touch. And whenever my stupid sight decides to come back, I'll be able to contribute a lot more around here. I don't make a half-bad grilled cheese either."

I heard his footsteps get closer, then his arms came around me, and he rested his chin on top of my head.

"Before you were released, Dr. Michaels told you that your sight could come back without any warning. The same way you lost it. And the cast is coming off in two days. Things will get back to normal...well, normal for you and me. But we're going to have to face the fact that we suck at the house shit. I now believe your mother was the one who kept us in line and from being complete slobs." We both laughed.

"Then what are we supposed to do?" I asked after we stopped laughing, and he let me go and went back to moving around the kitchen.

"First, we are going to Da Silva's for dinner.

Then tomorrow the search for a housekeeper begins. Hopefully, one who can cook and doesn't mind having that as part of the deal."

"Are you talking about a live-in housekeeper?"

"No, I think we could manage with someone Monday through Friday. Surely, we can survive the weekend on our own, don't you?"

"Yes. I think it's an awesome idea," I agreed. With someone here during the day, my dad wouldn't feel as if he needed to stay home with me. He'd only run into his office at the law firm a few times in the last five weeks. His cases had to be backing up even with his ability to work from his in-home office.

"What's the matter, Livi?"

"Nothing, I'm going to change my clothes," I answered, then stuck my arm out and turned in the direction where I knew the doorway was that led into the hallway.

"Okay. Yell if you need help finding anything."

I stopped with my hand on the doorframe. "I appreciate everything you have done for me, Dad. I'm sorry you have had to miss so much work to take care of me," I said, then started to feel my way down the hallway until I stopped when my dad's hands touched my shoulders.

He turned me. "You have nothing to be sorry for, Livi. I'm your dad and it is my job to take care of you. Besides, we both needed time to adjust. And please, missing work is one of the benefits of being a partner in the firm. We've been doing

73

alright, haven't we, Livi?"

"Yeah. I just wish everything were back to normal."

"We'll get there eventually."

"I love you, Dad."

"Love you, too, Livi."

After I reached my bedroom and changed clothes, then verified with my dad that what I had on matched before we left for the restaurant. It would be the first time going out for dinner without my mom. Sometimes it was hard to believe she'd been gone for over a month.

Maybe because we had had so much to do when we got home. Within a week after we had gotten back, we buried her. Then two days after her funeral, I began therapy. I wasn't sure if talking about everything that happened and the nightmares that had started, well...*the* nightmare because it was always the same one—the accident, was going to work.

Everyone around me thought talking about the accident would unlock whatever was keeping my sight from returning. I had to admit it helped with the nightmare because though I still had the same one, it wasn't *every* night. Next, I visited the orthopedic doctor to make sure my arm was healing correctly.

I was so over doctors.

I knew my dad and I needed to move on, but I missed my mom. My dad did, too. It wasn't like we would ever forget my mom, we just needed to learn to live without her. And to a point, I guess we were—one step, one hour, one day at a time.

"Oh, wow, I'm stuffed." I lifted the napkin from my lap and wiped my mouth, then sat it on the table.

"Does that mean you don't have room for dessert?" I groaned, and my dad chuckled. "I'll take that as a no."

"Definitely a no. Instead of leading me, you would have to roll me out of here if I ate a bit of anything else."

"Okay then, let me get the check paid, and we'll head home. We could pick up some ice cream for later?"

"Sure."

We debated what kind of ice cream we wanted while we waited for the waitress to bring my dad's card and receipt back.

"Here you go, sir. Have a nice evening," the waitress said.

"Thank you," my dad replied to the waitress. After she walked away, he asked me if I was ready.

"Yes, but can we stop at the ladies' room first?"

"Of course." Dad took hold of my elbow, helped me up from my chair, and then led me to the ladies' room. "Here we are, Livi. The door is in front of you. I'll be right here when you come out. If you need me just yell."

I might not be able to see with my eyes, but I could still roll them. My dad had been helping me since I left the hospital, but even with my disadvantage, no way I'd let him help me with private things. It would be too embarrassing. Probably for both of us.

"I think I can manage. Besides, it's the *ladies'* room."

"So what?"

"There could be other women inside who wouldn't take kindly to you walking in." I chuckled and pushed on the door.

"Like I'd give a shit what they, or anyone else, thought if you needed me."

Still holding the door open, I said, "You're the best dad ever."

"You know it and keep that in mind when I cook dinner tomorrow night."

I giggled as I let the door go. It took a few seconds of feeling around until I hit a stall door. I would be forever thankful we ate at Da Silva's quite a few times in the past, leaving me with some memory of how the restroom was set up.

After finishing my business, I moved to the sink to wash my hands, and when I put my hands under the water, I splashed some on my shirt. Turning the water off, I felt around in front of me for a paper towel dispenser. Yanking a few sheets out, I dried my hands, then patted the towel over the front of my shirt. With my elbow, I used the wall to guide me back in the direction of the door.

I found the door, grabbed the handle, swung it open, and said as I stepped out, "I got my shirt wet," and ran into a body. The force knocked me back just as the door closed, and I whacked the back of my head. My eyes closed, and I raised my good arm and rubbed the spot with my hand.

"Crap! Sorry, are you okay?" came from an unfamiliar voice.

At the same time, my dad said, "Christ, Livi!"

Embarrassed and wanting to be anywhere else, I ignored my dad and responded to the unknown person I attempted to plow over, "I think I'm the one who should be saying sorry."

"Nah, you're good. Did I hurt you? Are you in pain? You have your eyes squeezed shut," the voice spoke asked, and I caught an accent that definitely didn't belong to a lifetime resident of Boston.

"Livi, are you hurt?"

"No, Dad, just a little embarrassed," I said because all I needed was my dad freaking out and calling 911, making the whole experience more humiliating. "I'm fine. Can we go now?" I asked and dropped my hand, then opened my eyes. I blinked a couple of times before I shouted, "Oh my God, I can see you!" Then threw my arms around the guy in front of me, who I surmised was the one I bumped in to.

"Whoa, yeah, that's what happens when you open your eyes," was the response from the guy, which made me realize what I had done. I dropped

77

my arms and stepped back.

I was opened my mouth to apologize but found myself looking into the darkest brown eyes I had ever seen.

"Livi, what is wro—" Dad stopped before he finished his question and asked a different one, "Did you just say you can see?"

I turned my head in my dad's direction, breaking eye contact with the guy who I was sure thought I was crazy. "Yes," I answered, and my dad moved in and wrapped his arms around me.

I laid my face against his chest and let the tears fall. I don't know how long we stood there, but when my crying jag was over, I raised my head, and the guy with brown eyes was no longer in the hallway.

I leaned my head back and looked up at my dad and smiled. "If I had known a hit to the head would have fixed my sight, I would have done it sooner."

My dad laughed and squeezed me tight. "I'm don't care how it happened. I'm just so damn glad it came back," he said, then let me go. When I looked into his face again, I saw the moisture in his eyes. I wondered if he had feared like I had that my eyesight wouldn't return.

"Let's go home, Dad."

"Sounds like a good idea." My dad led me out of the restaurant and once in the car went straight to our house. He called the services for my therapist and our family doctor and left messages.

We hadn't even picked up ice cream. Instead, we celebrated with the single pre-packaged brownies from a box. They'd never tasted so good.

I took in everything on the car ride to the house. Once inside, I looked around as I walked through the house. Everything seemed brighter. My dad and I celebrated, then I made my way upstairs to my room. I had a new respect for anyone who suffered from permanently being blind or having any type of sight issues that kept you from experience the beauty of everything around you. For the rest of my life, I would be grateful for what I had, what I would experience, and what I would accomplish.

In my room, I touched the things on my dresser and ran my fingers over my violin case that was leaning in the corner by the bathroom door. I even watched myself in the mirror while I brushed my teeth as if it were a new experience.

Once in bed, I reached and turned the lamp off, then snuggled down under the covers. I closed my eyes with the knowledge that I'd never take any of my abilities for granted. You could lose one in the blink of your eyes.

Instead of the familiar nightmare, which only sometimes showed up, I stared into the dark brown eyes I had seen earlier. I was sure if I ever saw them again, I'd remember them and the guy they belonged to.

two paths *One* destiny

two paths One destiny

Chapter Nine

Lucio

I shut out everything in the gym except the familiar sound of the speed bag as it sprang back and forth. Keeping the rhythm going, I replayed the fight from two days ago in my head.

The crowd had been rowdy as they shouted for my opponent. They wanted him to win. Every time he landed a blow, they chanted his damn name. It grated on my last nerve. I knew better than to let the shit get into my head, but I had. Then I found myself struggling with the voice in the back of mind taunting that I'll never be good enough.

I'd spent the first two years in Boston getting used to my new life and graduating high school. My mom and I lived six months at my uncle's house until my mom had saved enough from her housekeeping job for us to afford a place of our own. I even worked at my uncle Tony's restaurant after I could move without grimacing from the slow healing of my ribs and up until I started making enough money with the small local fights. It had been another long three years, learning wrestling moves, taking martial art classes, working on my form, and building the stamina I would need for the ring. I started at the bottom of the MMA bouts with little to no pay. There were nights I crawled into bed and wondered if I'd ever reach the next level. Was I doomed to fail at everything? Spending my life running from past mistakes and wondering if I was fast enough to outrun what fate seemed to have in store for me.

I would have given up then, but I'd gotten the taste of being a winner, and it settled in me enough to stick with it. Even if only to prove to myself that I could do better. Oh, there'd been losses in my journey so far, and I used them and the feelings I had after losing to push myself harder. Because somewhere along the way, what I had started with the misguided notion it would keep me closer to my dad, had turned into my desire to prove I was in control of my future.

It'd taken some time, but the days, weeks, months, and years I'd worked to climb the ranks, was down to three fights. Three wins that would put me on top.

I sent the speed bag into motion again and thought about one of the fights.

At twenty-two—I'd taken the underdog status and used it to my advantage.

Ray Cabeara wasn't to be counted out as he sidestepped my punch and countered it with a kick that had his ankle and foot making contact with my right side at the kidney. The grunt and twinge to the side that I couldn't control, showed the blow had some power behind it.

He came for me and tried a grappling hold for a takedown to the mat, but I was ready for the move. Before Cabeara got close enough to get his arms around me, I sidestepped him. My quickness paid off and left him in a vulnerable position for my kick, which was delivered with precision and knocked him off balance. The bell rang as Cabeara righted himself.

"Better have enjoyed that lucky shot. You won't get another," Cabeara said and started toward his corner. I'd smiled when I noticed the slightly less exuberant way he walked.

The next three rounds had been brutal. Cabeara fought to keep his standing, and I fought to unseat him. Both of us sported marks on different areas of our bodies, and we would feel the effects of the bout for days after while our bodies healed.

It was what I was currently doing in the gym. Working out the soreness, so my body wouldn't get stiff.

In the last round of the fight with Cabeara, I had been ready. My body ached, but I knew if could *push the aside for a few more minutes, I would win the bout. I charged Cabeara low, wrapped my arms around his thighs, then lifted him up and brought us both down to the mat. I scrambled and tried to straddle Cabeara while throwing punches. Cabeara struggled to block the punches while he tried to toss me off.*

He bucked his hips, and I slipped off. Anticipating the move, I shuffled out of his reach and bounced to my feet. Time was ticking, and it was now or never.

We'd squared off again and we both threw punch for punch from each other. The crowd was vocal, and I lost a second of my focus, which gave Cabeara an opening. He stepped back to give himself a little room, and I watched as he rotated his hips. I knew the move. I'd seen him fight on more than one occasion. As he swung his leg out and aimed for my chin, I stepped back to gain enough space to counter. I grabbed Cabeara's leg and held it, keeping him off balance, but using him for my own. I swung my own leg forward as I twisted my hips. The blow contained enough force that when my foot met the side of Cabeara's head, he was done. I let go of his leg and he to the mat, unconscious.

"Weren't you supposed to be taking a couple days off? I ran by your place to see if you wanted to grab something to eat. When you didn't answer, I knew you'd be here." Tao's interruption brought me out of my head.

"I needed to burn off some energy and work out a little, so I don't get stiff. Why didn't you text?" I stopped the bag and stepped away.

Tao laughed. "Dude, there's a better way to burn energy without punishing your already bruised hands. The same activity will definitely relax your body, too. At least most of your body from going stiff." I shook my head, and Tao chuckled at his own joke before he continued. "And I didn't text because I figured you'd be lounging around and blow me off. When you weren't home, I knew there was only one other place you would be."

Tao was on staff as a trainer at the gym. Walt was my manager, and he owned the place. When I started competing, Tao began filling in as my sparring partner, too. We'd become fast friends. I tried not to overthink the fact he seemed to have the same easygoing demeanor Davis had.

"You're in a good mood. What did you do last night?" I asked as I unrolled the wraps from my hands. Tao was right, my knuckles were bruised and a little tender, but no way would I admit it to him.

"Please, you mean, *who* was I doing last night."

"You're such a ho," I said, followed by a groan, and shook my head as I tossed the strips in my opened bag on the floor. When I arrived at the gym, I hadn't even bothered to go to the locker room. I had dropped my bag, took out the wraps and after getting them on, I started in on the bag.

"Might loosen up your muscles and release some tension if you'd spend some time with a woman. You know, touch some soft skin... maybe get laid." I went to punch him, and he jumped out of the way and laughed.

I moved to the weight machines, and after placing the weight plates I needed on the ends, I sat on the bench and started with my legs.

"I released tension two days ago. It's how I obtained the sore muscles in the first place."

"If you think a fight compares to touching, caressing, and getting sweaty with a woman...I'm going to suggest a doctor take a look inside your head. Damn, Lucio, what happened to the blonde you were dating with the legs up to her ears. What was her name, Lucy, Laney, Lindy, or something else that starts with an L?"

The weights clanged as I let them down and swung my legs around on the bench. "Lynn. And that ended two months ago."

"Seriously?"

"Yeah, she started giving me grief about how much time I spent training. And evidently, when I have a bout scheduled, I'm so focused I don't pay attention to anything else. Mainly her."

"Tough break she walked."

"All's good," I said and stood. I didn't want to share it been a huge argument and that Lynn hadn't walked, I'd told her to get out. Her parting shot was she hoped Cabeara beat the shit out of me because I was an asshole who would never amount to anything. Of course, I came back with, "Then it's a good thing you're on the way out and don't have to worry about me dragging you down."

After she left my apartment, I grabbed the Chinese takeout bag I'd brought home and a beer and ate in the living room, watching sports. She'd lasted longer than any other woman I'd dated. Maybe Tao's one and done attitude wasn't a bad thing. No attachment, no worry you're not giving them enough attention. But in my defense, Lynn wanted me to be invested in her life when the only thing she'd cared about was bragging rights of dating an MMA fighter. The steady sex was missed, though.

"I'm going to go grab some food. Want me to bring you something back?" Tao asked, and the subject of women dropped thankfully.

"Yeah, if you don't mind. I want to finish my workout." I leaned and reached into my bag for my wallet. As I pulled it out, I noticed my cell blinking indicating I'd missed a call or text. Swiping the screen, I saw my mom's number and that she left a voicemail. "Hold on a second. My mom never leaves a message when she calls."

"She's at work, right?"

"Should be," I answered as I hit the button and listened to the message. Relieved it wasn't anything major. I texted her, looked at the time on the screen, then dropped the phone back in my bag. "I have to pick her up at six. Something's wrong with her car. Uncle Tony swung by this morning and dropped her off at work, but he won't be able to pick her up because it'll be the dinner rush at the restaurant."

"Hell, you'd think the people she works for would offer. Hasn't she worked for the same family since right after you guys moved here?" Tao questioned as he took the cash I held out for my food.

"She's been with them for, I don't know, maybe five and a half or six years. Yeah, it wasn't long after we moved here. Even with that, if they volunteered, Mom would never accept. She'd feel like she was imposing."

"So, what are you in the mood for? I'm thinking of a big, greasy burger and fries."

I cringed. "I can hear your arteries hardening. How about subs and you can even get chips with yours? You get carbs, starch, and protein minus the grease. Cut your body a break, man. You do work in a gym."

"You're actually going to eat a sub and chips?" He snorted in disbelief because I rarely indulged in any fast food. Not that I didn't eat out, I did. But even cheating, I tried to stick with healthier choices and not overindulge.

"No chips for me. But I'll take two twelve-inch turkey, with extra serving on meat only. And have them toast the wheat bread."

Tao rolled his eyes. "Christ, now I know why I went the trainer route, instead of becoming a fighter."

"I thought it was because you didn't want your pretty face abused."

"True. I mean, look at your face. You have a cut over one eye, a cheek that is still a little puffy and doesn't know what shade it wants to be, and I'm not even going to go over the rest of your body. Seriously, the one kick you took to the side, I'm surprised you're not pissing blood. No thanks. The headgear is the only reason I spar with you."

"Whatever. Go grab our food. I'm going to hit the treadmill."

"Run a mile for me," Tao said, then headed for the door as I walked toward the machine. Once I finished my workout, then ate, it'd still leave plenty of time to chill out at my apartment before I had to pick up my mom.

After jogging to my car and fighting traffic from Roxbury Crossing to Beacon Hill, I reached the street and the house where my mom worked. Running only ten minutes late. I never should've laid down when I got home from the gym.

I realized as I pulled up to the house that in the time my mom worked here, I never been to the home. Not to drop her off or pick her up. I was also surprised my mom wasn't outside tapping her foot and miffed that I was late.

I parked behind the car that sat in front of the house and jumped out, grabbing the shirt I'd picked up on my way out my apartment.

The house was large, but it didn't surprise me. Beacon Hill was a high-end area. I rang the bell, and the door was answered immediately as my head popped through the no sleeves t-shirt.

"Sorry," I said as I pulled the shirt down over my torso, then turned my attention to the person who had opened the door. I was caught off guard when it wasn't my mom standing there. I expected her to be the one at the door—not the brown-haired, brown-eyed young woman who stood in front of me.

When I glanced down, she was staring at me but hadn't said a word.

"Umm, I'm here to pick up my mom." I lifted a brow in question as she continued to stare.

Finally, she shook her head as if clearing it out and spoke, "Oh, yes. You must be Gina's son."

"That'd be me. If you tell Mom, I'm here, I'll wait for her in the car."

"No. No," the young woman said in a hurried tone, then stepped to the side. "Please come in. She's in the kitchen." Then her cheeks started to pinken as her eyes stayed focused on my face.

"You're probably wondering about my face being a bit banged up, huh? I had a fight the other day."

"A fight?"

I laughed at how she said it and the expression that appeared on her face.

"A sanctioned fight. Not a punch someone for

no reason street fight. I'm an MMA fighter." I stepped past her and into the house.

"Oh," she replied, then smiled and pointed. "The kitchen is that way."

As I walked down the hallway her footsteps followed behind me. I made a mental note to ask my mom if the woman had something wrong with her. Not that it mattered, I just never remembered my mom mentioning anything about her before. But then again, it's not like we talked about her job past the question of how her day went.

The thought entered my mind that Lynn was right, and I didn't pay attention to anything other than training and my next fight. Because I knew nothing about the family my mom worked for other than the man was an attorney.

Christ, I'd kept everything and everyone around me at a distance for so long. A part of me was afraid I'd lose anyone I let get too close to me. Suddenly it hit me that even though I worked to change the course of my life, it didn't mean I had to do it alone. Maybe that was why I always felt as if something was missing from my life.

Like the missing part was the key to making everything in my life fall into place.

two paths *O*ne destiny

Chapter Ten

Olivia

After being upstairs in my room, going over sheet music for an hour, I headed downstairs for a much needed break. As I reached the halfway point on the stairs, the aroma of food hit me, and my stomach growled. Whatever Gina had cooked smelled delicious.

With my mind on the food as I reached the landing, the doorbell startled me. So much so, that I swung the door open without a second thought to who could be on the other side. Then I stood frozen to my spot and struggled to gain my speech because of the man on the stoop in the process of pulling a shirt over his head.

It didn't take him long to get the sleeveless t-shirt pulled down, but I'd gotten a fair glimpse of him. Enough to notice that he was in shape. Excellent shape. His chest was toned with some

95

hair, and his arms were muscled. He had a six-pack that led to a tapered waist and a trail of brown hair that ran down and into the waistband of the pair of black gym shorts he wore.

When he spoke, I had to look up to view his face. Even with a cut above one eye and what looked like a bruise on his cheek, he was good looking. Beautiful in fact, but I didn't think he'd appreciate that sentiment if I spoke it out loud. Not that I gained the ability to speak. His hair was brown and cut short on the sides with the top layer pulled back in a small ponytail. The hair on his face was the same shade of brown and it was short and neat.

The man was the full package, but his eyes were what mesmerized me the most. They were a rich dark brown and they had a warmness to them.

He was staring at me with his eyebrow cocked and I realized he must have spoken again. I shook my head and tried to recall what he said. Something about picking up his mom.

"Oh, yes. You must be Gina's son." I remembered Gina had mentioned her car hadn't started that morning and her son would be picking her up. Dad and I both had offered to take her home whenever she was finished that evening, but she had declined.

When Dad had hired Gina, and she first came to work for us, I'd been fifteen and called her Mrs. Moretti. After she'd been with us a year, she insisted we call her Gina because she considered us as her second family. Which I guessed wasn't far off since she spent Monday through Friday from seven in the morning to six in the evening at our house. She might have been hired as a housekeeper, but she quickly became a godsend for my dad and me. We both were struggling with the loss of my mom and hadn't realized how much until Gina had stepped into our lives. She hadn't walked in and tried to take over the place. She just quietly went about doing what needed done. Her kindness and warmth had made it easier for my dad and I to get through the days.

"That'd be me. If you would tell my mom, I'm here, I'll wait for her in the car."

"No. No," I answered quickly, not ready to let Gina's son leave my presence. "Please come in. She's in the kitchen." I stepped to the side to give him space to come through the door and waved my hand toward the direction of the kitchen. I hoped his mom was in the kitchen. I wasn't sure, but she'd have to be somewhere in the house.

I felt the heat rise on my cheeks and prayed he hadn't notice as I continued to stare at his face while I waited for him to walk in. He seemed a little familiar to me, which was odd because even though Gina mentioned having a son, I'd never met him. He never been to the house in the years his mom worked here.

"You're probably wondering about my face being a bit banged up, huh? I had a fight the other day."

I wanted to laugh because it hadn't even crossed my mind. I'd been too busy ogling the guy's body. So, to cover, I blurted out, "A fight?"

He laughed. "A sanctioned fight. Not a punch someone for no reason street fight. I'm an MMA fighter," he said as he stepped past me.

"Oh," I replied, then smiled and pointed. "The kitchen is that way."

He gave me one last look before he started down the hallway. I closed the front door and followed. Neither of us said anything. The poor guy probably thought something was wrong with me. I didn't speak on the way to the kitchen because the view from the back was as impressive as the front. He had a nice tight butt that I suddenly wanted to squeeze to see just how firm it was. The thought had heat rising on my face.

For God's sake, I was twenty-one years old. I'd dated before. First, as a teenager and then as an adult. By no means would I be considered experienced, considering I only dated two men that had been for longer than a couple of times out on dates. And I'd only had sex with one. Dean. Probably because we were both students at Berklee and majoring in Music Performance. I'd broken it off with him six months ago when he talked about moving in together and both of us auditioning for the Boston Symphony as if he had our future planned out.

I knew then I needed to make the break. I liked Dean; we had a lot in common. The sex with him

98

was okay, but he was my only reference, so maybe that was as good as it got. But something always felt off with our relationship, not like creepy wise or bad, more as if I were missing something in my life—a part of me. It was hard to explain even to myself, and I mentioned none of it to Dean in our breakup. Instead, I just told him I wasn't ready. When he said okay, and nothing needed to change that we could still be a couple, and one day he was sure I would be ready to commit.

I hadn't been sure how to take his response, so I used the old cliché about needing time and we should take a break. Dean hadn't been happy, but he agreed to it. Yet, at least once a month, he asked me if I had had enough time to myself and was ready to take the next step in our relationship. His actions and tone had sent up a red flag and I had ended it.

"Lucio!" Gina's voice snapped me out of my head and my eyes off her son's cute butt.

"Hey, Mom. Sorry about running late. I laid down after the gym and I dozed off." I smiled when he bent over and kissed the top of his mom's head.

"It's no problem. I used the extra time to write a grocery list." She patted his shoulder.

"Olivia, you met Lucio, my son?" she asked as she picked the list up off the counter and shoved the sheet of paper in her purse.

"Shit, I'm sorry," he said and offered his hand. "I'm Lucio." Then he smirked and winked at me when his mom popped him on the shoulder and told him not to curse.

I took his offered hand, tried to ignore the zap of electricity as our hands touched, and said, "Olivia or Livi. I answer to both." I smiled back at him.

"Nice to meet you...Livi." He held my hand a little longer after we shook, and I felt a loss when he released it.

"You ready, Mom?"

"Yes," she answered Lucio, then turned to me. "Olivia, there's a chicken casserole warming in the oven. It should be alright until your dad gets home."

"Thank you, Gina. It smells wonderful. Dad better be home soon, or I may have to eat before he gets here."

She laughed and hugged me. "I'll see you in the morning."

"Have a nice evening," I said as she and Lucio started to walk out of the kitchen.

Lucio stopped and turned around. "Bye, Livi. Nice meeting you."

"You, too. Bye," I replied and stood looking at the empty doorway until I heard the front door close.

"Get a grip, Livi. You probably won't ever see him again. He only showed up today because of his mom," I said out loud to the empty kitchen. I grabbed a bottle of water out of the refrigerator and walked into the family room. My dad would be home soon, and then we'd eat.

The bell rang again, and I changed directions and headed toward the front door. When I swung the door open, Lucio stood there.

"Hey, long time no see," he joked, and we both laughed. "Sorry, Mom said she left her grocery list on the counter.

"She—" I stopped myself before I told him I saw her put it in her shoulder bag. Was it wrong I wanted to be around him for a couple more minutes? "Let's go look." I closed the door behind him, and we walked to the kitchen.

"Hmm, it isn't on the counter," he said, then turned around to face me. "It probably fell to the bottom in that thing the woman calls a purse. It's bigger than my gym bag."

"Hey, in her defense, we women need certain things at our disposal."

"Yeah, okay. Not sure how many times you need a handheld can opener, six packs of tissues, half a dozen rubber bands, eight paperclips. One time when she told me to get something out of her bag, I saw a pair of earrings and a pair of nylon hose. Ever catch a rerun of that old show, MacGyver?"

"Yes," I said and chuckled.

"She's the female version. I'm surprised she didn't fix her car this morning. She probably has what she needs in there to do it."

"Be nice."

"I can be, but sometimes being bad is more fun." The way he said it and looked at me, I shivered. When I looked into his eyes, I saw his interest in me. I wasn't sure I had the skills or experience to handle a guy like him. And wasn't that sad considering he couldn't be that much older than me. But there was something behind his eyes when I stared into them that said he had experienced more in life than I had.

"I better go before she comes in looking for me," he said but didn't move to leave. "I'm meeting a friend later, and we're going to check out the House of Blues club. Want to come?"

"Umm..." I said while I mentally ran tomorrow's schedule through my head.

"Hey, no biggie if you don't want to go. We just met. I get it," Lucio said, and I assumed it was because I paused in answering.

"No, it isn't that. I want to go. I was going over my schedule. I don't have class in the morning, and practice isn't until three."

"Whoa, class? Please tell me you aren't in high school, and practice isn't for like cheerleading or some shit."

I probably should have been offended, but I wasn't. I smiled. "No, I go to Berklee, and practice is for BCSO. I'm twenty-one."

"That's a relief. What's BCSO?"

"The Berklee Contemporary Symphony Orchestra. I play the violin."

"No shit."

"No shit," I repeated, and for the first time, he looked embarrassed.

"Sorry."

"Don't be. I've never been to the House of Blues. What should I wear? Is it dressy or casual?"

"Casual. Not that I'll complain if you want to dress up." He looked me up and down, then grinned. "Especially if you want to wear a little black dress or skirt. With heels."

God, he was hot when he flirted.

"I'll find something."

"Lucio, I found the list!" Gina yelled from the front door.

"Okay, Mom," he said loudly, then looked down at me. "I'll swing by around nine."

"I could meet you there," I offered, not knowing where he lived and if picking me up would be a hassle for him.

"It's not a problem. I wasn't asking you to come hang out. It's a date, Livi. Besides, I wouldn't want you to drive alone to the club."

"Oh." Another show of how out of my element I was. My stomach tightened when he mentioned it was for a date. However, he had mentioned a friend. "Are you sure it will be okay with your friend?"

"Tao, yeah. And if he tries to hit on you, I'll punch him." He winked.

"Does he normally hit on your dates?"

He grinned. "Tao hits on all women. You'll actually be saving me from sitting alone most of the night or having to leave alone."

"Why?"

"Because Tao usually hook-ups and cuts out on me."

"Ah, so he's a man-whore?" I laughed when his eyes went wide.

"Nailed it," he said and started toward the front door. When we reached the door, he opened it but didn't walk out.

"Something wrong?" I asked, and he reached out and cupped my cheek.

"I might be headed for trouble with you," Lucio said, then dropped his hand and walked to his car where his mom was in the passenger seat waiting for him.

After I watched them pull away, I closed the door and leaned against it, and reached up and touched my cheek where his hand had been.

"The feeling is mutual," I whispered, then smiled when I remembered something my mom said to me.

'Choose your husband wisely, Olivia. Bad boys may be exciting and seem like all that, but as you grow older, trust me, they tend to test your last nerve.' She had been joking with my dad at the time.

I pushed off the door and headed back toward the kitchen. "I don't know about marriage, Mom, or if I'm ready for a bad boy, but I'm fixing to find out."

I laughed, opened the oven, and pulled the casserole out.

104

Chapter Eleven

Lucio

As soon as I slid into the driver's seat of my car, I glanced at my mom. The look on her face told me she'd witnessed what happened with Livi. She verified I was right as soon as I pulled away from the curb. I just didn't expect the anger.

"What in the hell was that about, Lucio?"

"I'm not sure." It was not the right answer for my mom.

"You're not sure! I swear to God, Lucio, if you toy with her, I will come to your apartment and smother you in your sleep!"

Not only had I misspoken, but I laughed. There wasn't even a need to glance over because I felt my mom's eyes boring into me.

After I got my laughter under control, I said, "I asked her out, Mom." When my mom didn't reply, I cut my eyes to her. She wasn't looking at me, she was looking out the passenger's side window. "Mom?"

"I heard you, Lucio."

"You're not going to yell some more and tell me to stay away from her? Or that she's probably too good for me?"

Minutes went by before I heard her blow out a breath and then shift in her seat.

"No, I'm not going to yell nor tell you to stay away from Olivia."

"But you do think she's too good for me?" I asked and not going to lie—a little hurt that my mom would think that.

Hell, I knew it two seconds after Livi opened the door that she was way to innocent for the likes of me. When I stood in the kitchen and asked if she wanted to go to the club and she'd had no idea I was talking about a date. But what brought it home for me was when she explained about her classes and practice. She was college, I was street. She was a violinist in an orchestra, and I used my fists to make a living. Could we be more opposite from each other? Yet, knowing it hadn't stopped me from flirting with her. And it hadn't kept me from asking her out. I felt comfortable around her, and I acted like I hadn't felt the zap when our hands touched because I hadn't wanted to embarrass myself. But I'd never experienced anything like it before.

She'd felt it, too. She was easy to read and tiny jolt from her was a dead giveaway. At the door, it was the reason I said I might be headed for trouble with her. I might have just met her, but I knew deep down if I let her in and something went wrong between us or happened to her—it'd break me. Knowing she had the ability scared the hell out of me.

My mom sat quietly until I pulled up in front of her apartment building. When I stopped the car and turned to look at her, she spoke, "I don't like it when you talk about not being good enough. Have you had your moments? Yes. I watched a boy who always took others' feelings into account, turn into a teenager I didn't recognize or understand. Your dad and I felt helpless when you started hanging around with Travis' crew. We watched you get deeper and deeper, and there was nothing we could do to stop it but continue to love you and pray we wouldn't lose you to some senseless gang activity."

I opened my mouth, but she raised her hand and stopped me.

"We've never spoken about what went on once we moved here, and that was my fault. I didn't want to dredge up any of it because I was still raw from your dad's death. Then after the hurt eased, you were settling in here, studying to catch up in school, even working part-time at the restaurant. I was getting my son back and feared if we dredged everything up, it might have a reverse effect. I couldn't go through that again. Losing your dad, then getting the call that you were being

107

taken to the hospital and not knowing anything other than you'd been shot and thinking I might lose you, too. No way I wanted to go back and revisit any of it.

"Then you graduated high school, and decided you were going to go into the MMA. I'll admit I figured you'd lose interest, or maybe I hoped you'd lose interest. I wanted you to attend college, get a better education than your dad and I had. Parents always want their children to do better than them.

"But you didn't want to go to college, so I watched you work and push yourself, and the single-minded focus you held. That was when I knew you'd found your place. As a mother, I don't like seeing you with bruises and cuts or swollen knuckles and I probably never get used to it. However, I do enjoy seeing the enthusiasm and love for the sport in your eyes when you talk about it."

"The money helps," I said, and she smiled.

"Right. When you first started, you barely made enough to pay your rent. If you hadn't pulled shifts at Da Silva's, you wouldn't have eaten unless you came by the house."

I snorted, but my mom was right. The only thing there's plenty of when you start out in the MMA is soreness and bruises.

"Not anymore. My take on the last fight was more than I've made with all the other fights added together and then some."

"Thank you for reminding me. I noticed a

deposit this morning in my bank account. We'll talk about that later. You're getting me off track."

"Oh, there's a point to what you've been saying?"

"Luca Lucio Moretti, you aren't so big I can't turn you over my knee."

She smacked my arm when I laughed. The woman was at best five feet four and maybe a hundred thirty, and that was being generous on my part. Where I was six three and two-forty.

"I may have taken the long way around to get to my point, but things need to be said. You're my son, and I will always love you. Olivia is a beautiful, talented young woman, but Lucio, she isn't as...experienced in life as you. Though you do have something in common, you've both lost a parent. Tragically, too. Your dad was shot and killed. Her mother died in a terrible accident with Olivia in the car to witness it. Its why Mr. Chambers was looking to hire a housekeeper. The house had been his wife's domain. He and Olivia were having a hard time maintaining the house and their lives without her. So please just be gentle with her. And for God's sake, if you are looking for just a hookup, then stay clear. I love my job, and Olivia and her dad are wonderful people."

"Geez, Mom."

"Don't geez me. I'm not blind. I've seen the girls you and Tao...associate with."

"Fine," I answered because there was no sense in arguing with her. And laughing would only keep her going. Besides, she'd nailed Tao, but I wasn't nearly as bad as he was, and I refused to have this discussion with my her.

"Be a gentleman, Lucio. Don't forget dinner Sunday for your birthday," she said and opened her door.

"I won't. Please don't go all out cooking. And no cake."

"Pfft, one slice isn't going to kill you. You'll work it off at the gym, I'm sure." I leaned over and kissed her cheek before she slid out of the car.

"Just all the other fatting foods you're going to have me eat."

"Go and shower and dress nice for your date," she said and got out of the car. "I'm proud of you," she added, then closed the door.

I smiled and watched as she headed toward the door of her building. Then I rolled down the window.

"Mom, I forgot about your car. Do you need me to look at it, or have it picked up and taken to a garage?"

"No. I meant to tell you that your uncle Tony sent someone to look at it after he dropped me at work. It only needed a new battery, so the man who came by swapped it out."

"Okay. Love ya, Mom."

"Love you, Lucio."

Once she went through the door, I drove away. I replayed everything we talked about and wondered if I shouldn't call Livi and cancel. Just the thought it might disappoint or hurt her feelings had me pushing the idea away. By the time I walked into my apartment, I was actually looking forward to seeing her again. Though I decided it was best if I didn't touch her.

My mom said she loved her job and the Chambers. I wouldn't jeopardize that because of a little flare of electricity. I'd been busy the last few months getting prepared for the fight and hadn't so much as considered spending time with a woman. Especially since Lindy was gone. Hell, maybe Tao was right, I needed to get laid, and Livi was gorgeous and piqued my interest. That was probably where all my interest was coming from.

I stepped into the shower and under the spray of hot water, pleased I'd thought it out before making a decision with the potential to hurt more than one person.

When Livi opened the door, every single thought I had about placing her in the no-touch zone had been a wasted effort on my part.

She wore black jeans that hugged her curves, a white blouse unbuttoned at the top just enough to see her necklace. Her hair hung down in loose curls. She stood taller, which had me looking down to her feet, and my lips twitched at the black boots that only hit her ankles but had at least a three-inch heel. Spiked no less. Earlier she'd been in sweats and an oversized t-shirt, and though she'd looked good, the outfit hadn't done her justice.

I was fucked and not in a good way.

"Hi," she said.

"Hey, you ready?" I asked after I found my voice.

"Yes, just let me grab my bag. Come in, it'll only take me a second. I left it upstairs in my room." She held open the door, and I stepped in. "Do you want anything to drink?"

"No, I'm good, thanks. I'll wait here for you."

"Okay, be right back."

I watched her walk up the stairs and took a deep breath. It was going to be a long night for me. Keeping my hands off her was going to be tough. I'd wanted to shove my hands in her hair, then kiss her until neither of us could breathe. Then text Tao and blow him off, take her to my apartment and strip her of everything but those damn boots.

"You must be Lucio."

I turned at the man's voice. And prayed I didn't have drool on my chin or that he could read thoughts because I didn't think Livi's dad would appreciate either.

I stuck out my hand. "Yes, sir. Nice to meet you, Mr. Chambers."

"Call me, Richard," he said as he shook my hand. "When Livi said she was going out with Gina's son, I realized in we've never met. Hiring your mother was one of the best decisions I've ever made. She whipped Livi and I in shape along with the house."

"Mom's good at doing that."

"And you're Tony Da Silva's nephew, right?"

"Yes," I said and glanced over to the staircase, wishing Livi would appear. I knew her dad was an attorney, and it seemed he was in questioning mode. It wasn't like I had anything to hide. I just wasn't used to meeting a parent on the first date. Hell, I'd never even met Lynn's in the six months we were together.

"Nice man. My firm just handled the paperwork for his new restaurant."

"Yeah, he's pretty happy about the location of this one. The grand opening is next month. But it's not like I'll get to enjoy the food unless there are leftovers when it closes," I said and chuckled. "Uncle Tony will get upset if I snatch a sample while working."

"You work for Tony?" he asked and frowned, which confused me.

"I only fill in when he needs me now. But I've worked on and off for him since I was sixteen after my mom and I moved here."

His frown deepened as he stared at me. Then his expression changed, and he shook his head.

"I knew you looked familiar. You're older, taller, and filled out more. The facial hair threw me off, too. But it's you."

"Excuse me?" I said more confused than I'd been a second ago.

"Livi ran into you, literally, when she walked out of the ladies' room at Da Silva's. It's something like six years."

I frowned, then gave Mr. Chambers a once over. I'd only seen him for a few minutes in the hallway that led to the restrooms.

"Livi was the girl who hugged me for knocking her into the bathroom door?"

"Yes," he answered, then yelled, "Livi!"

I glanced toward the staircase, and Livi stood halfway down. She was smiling with her bag clutched against her chest.

"I heard," she said, and I watched as she walked the rest of the way down. And when she reached the landing, she did the same as she had in front of the bathroom—she threw her arms around me.

Chapter Twelve

Olivia

"I hope your friend wasn't mad we stood him up," I said as I handed him a glass of water, then sat down on the opposite end of the couch from him.

"Nah, he's good. When I texted him, I'd told him I'd explain later."

"I just feel bad."

"Don't. As long as there are single women in the club, he won't even miss us."

I laughed. "I can't believe Tao is that bad."

"Believe it," he said and took a drink of the water. He'd drank one beer with my dad when the three of us had moved to the family room to talk about the revelation from earlier. My dad had stayed in the room for a while, then claimed he had work to look over in his office, leaving Lucio and I alone.

Lucio had been the one to suggest we forgo the club and then texted his friend. He generally seemed as surprised as my dad and I to find out we had somewhat met before and the circumstances that surrounded my reaction to him outside the ladies' room.

I was unable to believe it was him from that day. Especially when I'd vowed, I'd never forget the eyes I'd looked into when my sight first returned. I'd even seen them in my dreams for months after. Maybe it was because I'd been fascinated with his body when he showed up to pick up his mom. Or it could have easily been his firm butt in those shorts. It had definitely captured my attention.

"You sure you wouldn't rather have soda or another beer?"

"No, really, I'm good. I limit myself to one beer when I do drink, and I can't tell you the last time I drank a soda."

"I wish I could be as disciplined," I said and then lifted my glass with Pepsi in it and drank.

"I have splurge days. But if I'm going to be on top in my weight class, I have to stay on track. I imagine you are disciplined with your music, right?"

"I am. I want to be part of the violin section in the Boston Symphony. That's my goal. I'm going to apply for an audition after I finish college. I have one semester left."

"I don't know much about orchestra music other than they play a lot of old stuff."

"It isn't all old stuff. The orchestra I'm part of now at Berklee, we play contemporary pieces. Even the big orchestras today play some modern selections. Now, I'm going to have to invite you to a concert so you can see, or should I say, hear what you've been missing."

"You're on. But only if I can get you to a fight," Lucio countered, then chuckled when I scrunched my nose.

"I'm not sure I can watch two men fight. Let alone make each other bleed," I said, then scooted closer to him and reached out. "This had to have hurt," I added as I gently ran my fingertips over the healing cut above his eyebrow.

"Not much. Your adrenaline runs high in a fight, so until it's over and the adrenaline nosedives, you don't feel much pain. After is a different story. And depending on whether you win or lose—depends on how much the pain affects you," he said. "Livi."

"Hmm," I answered as I expanded my exploration and ran my fingers down, caressing over the bruise on his cheek. "I count five colors inside this."

When he didn't say anything, I cut my eyes to his, and what I saw made my stomach tighten. I realized then that I had unintentionally moved myself even closer to him with my need to examine the marks on his face.

He lifted his arms and shoved his hands in my hair and cradle my head. The thumb on his left

117

hand ran over my lips, and I sucked in my breath, holding it. Anticipating his kiss. Wanting it.

"I need you to say no if you don't want me to kiss you. And if you don't want me to, please scoot back some. I'm afraid if you don't, I may kiss you regardless of whether you say no."

I moved my hand from his face and rested it on his chest, then leaned in until our noses almost touched.

"Is yes an option?" I'd wonder later where the bold woman had come from.

He pulled me closer, closing the gap and tilting his head slightly, so our noses wouldn't collide. When his lips touched mine, I wasn't sure what I expected, but his lips were soft yet firm. He pushed his tongue against the crease of my lips, and when I opened them, his tongue dove in.

Had I ever been kissed like this? I surely would have remembered, right?

His hands moved from my hair to my hips, and while he devoured my mouth, he shifted us until I straddled his hips. Once he had me where he wanted me, his hands roamed up and down my back.

I clutched at his shirt, then pulled my hands from between us, placing them on each side of his head. Holding him in place. My heart raced as he pulled me into him until our chest were pressed together.

Overrun with a feeling of need, I rotated my hips, then grinded against his hardness. His hand slid to my butt, and he held me down, my core heated as his hardness pressed against me. All thoughts vanished while my desire flourished.

He broke the kiss and rested his forehead against mine. "We need to stop, Livi. I don't want your dad walking in and find me mauling his daughter," he said breathing a little heavily, and I was glad I wasn't the only one fighting for air. Then his words registered.

"Oh my God, how could I have forgotten about my dad down the hall?" I felt his chest vibrate. "Are you laughing?"

He raised his head and grinned. "I was listening for footsteps when I first started kissing you. I pulled away because when you grinded down on me, I lost my hearing. Fairly sure a couple of more minutes in and an earthquake could have rocked Boston and I wouldn't have given a shit," he said, and I giggled when he lifted me off and plopped me down away from him.

He stood and adjusted himself. "Problem?" I asked and wondered who'd taken over my body because I wasn't flirty or bold when it came to men.

"I'm going home, smarty pants. It's late. I'm sure your dad wants to go to bed."

"He went to his office to work."

"He works past midnight in his office after pulling a full day?"

I laughed. "No."

"There you go. Now walk me to the door."

We walked out of the family room and into the hallway. We hadn't taken five steps when my dad popped out of his office. "You headed home, Lucio?"

"Yes, sir. Thanks for the beer. I'm sorry I stayed so late."

"All's good. It was nice to finally get an opportunity to thank you and explain what had happened. I remember you were as shellshocked as we were. You just didn't know the reason behind it. Drive safe, son."

"I will."

"Livi, let me know when you've locked the front door, and I'll arm the alarm," my dad said as Lucio and I stopped at the front door and my dad headed up the stairs.

"Hey, you got plans Sunday?" Lucio asked.

"No."

"Want to come with me to my mom's? She's cooking dinner."

"I wouldn't want to intrude?"

"You won't be intruding. Ask Mom tomorrow if it makes you feel better. You'll actually be helping me out because she will make a ton of food and a triple-layered cake. If you're there, she won't try to force it all on me."

I shook my head with a grin on my face. "Okay."

"Great, I'll pick you up around noon then. On Sundays, she likes to serve the big meal early. That's not a problem for you, is it?"

"Not at all. I'll see you Sunday."

"Bye, Livi," he said, then leaned down and kissed me on the cheek. When he rose, he pulled the door open and walked through it. As he was pulling it shut behind him, he added, "Don't forget to lock the door."

I locked the door, then went to the family room and picked up our glasses, turning off the lights in the room. After I set the glasses in the sink, I headed for the stairs. Once upstairs, I let my dad know everything was shut down and locked up, then made my way to my room.

After my nightly ritual was done, I slid into my bed. Instead of going to sleep, I laid there and thought about how strange life could be. When my eyelids grew heavy, I closed them and thought of a pair of brown eyes and the man associated with them.

Every minute I was around him, I liked him more. He was easy to talk to, and easy to be around. I couldn't wait to see him again.

two paths *One* destiny

Chapter Thirteen

Lucio

With my hand on Livi's lower back, I led her inside the building where my mom lived. It hadn't escaped me that when I was near her, I wanted to touch her. As if I needed the contact.

"Did you explain to Tao why we didn't go to the nightclub?"

"Yeah," I gave the one-word answer because I didn't want to think about the other night. If I did, I'd ultimately fast forward to our heated first kiss. I didn't want to walk into my mom's place with a hard-on.

It was bad enough I'd gotten so worked up from kissing her that night, I went home, took a shower and jacked off to the thoughts of her.

The next day at the gym, Tao asked what had happened, reminding me I promised to fill him in. So, I told him what happened. He hadn't found it the least bit odd that Livi and I had this weird roundabout connection before we met.

Instead, he'd laughed, slapped his thigh and stated it was fate. Then he went on to tell me I was doomed, and I'd shoved him. Then today when Livi opened the door and looked at me, I wondered if Tao was right. The bastard for placing that in my head.

"This is a nice place. Does Gina like living here?" Livi asked and looked up at me.

"She loves it. She moved here after I moved out of the other place. She still has two bedrooms here, but the overall square footage is smaller and easier for her to take care of. A bonus was that all the residents in the building are either her age or older. If you see a kid or two around here, they're definitely someone's grandkids."

"How did the night at the club go for Tao?" she asked, then giggled. She wasn't going to drop the subject. Then again, she wasn't the one drudging memories up that would give any man a stiffy. I smacked her on the butt because I could and snickered when she jumped and said not so quietly, "Hey, what was that for?"

"For wanting to know if my man-ho of a best friend found himself a hookup." When we were at my mom's door, I flipped the keys on my keyring to find the one to her door.

"You shouldn't call him that. I bet it hurts his feelings," Livi scolded as I reached out to put the key in the lock, but before I could, the door opened.

"Good grief. Were you planning to stand in the hall all day and talk," my mom commented as she pulled the door open wider.

"Hey, Mom, it was Livi holding us up," I said and gave Livi a little shove through the door.

"How is it my fault? It's not like I had the key to Gina's door. You did." I grinned at her indignant tone.

"You were distracting me with your questions?"

"Alright. Quit picking on Olivia, Lucio," my mom said, and when I looked at Livi, she stuck her tongue out at me.

I caught myself before I said, *Mom*, like a five-year-old. Instead, I waited until my mom turned toward Livi, then I did the adult thing and lifted my middle finger at her. She giggled, and my mom glanced over her shoulder at me. I shrugged as if I had no clue what was going on.

Mom shook her head at me before she turned back to Livi. "Dinner's ready, I was just waiting for you two to get here before I set it on the table. What can I get you to drink, sweetie?"

"Whatever you have is fine," Livi answered.

"How's Pepsi? I picked a six-pack up when I went to the store. I know you like it."

"You didn't have to do that, Gina."

"It was no trouble. Lucio, seat Olivia, then come in the kitchen and get everyone's drinks while I get the food."

I pulled out a chair for Olivia and couldn't help but bend down and whisper in her ear, "You'll pay later for sticking your tongue out at me." Then I bit her earlobe. After I received the reaction I wanted, a slight shiver, I walked away.

In the kitchen, I grabbed glasses and fixed the drinks. After a few trips back and forth, the three of us sat down to a meal of fried chicken, mashed potatoes and gravy, two vegetables, and homemade rolls. I dug in with the knowledge I would be putting a little more time in on my workout to compensate. It was okay to have a couple cheat days, but even on those days, I still tried to make good choices. But the extra workout time was worth not hurting my mom's feelings when she'd taken her time to cook for my birthday.

"Thank you for dinner, Gina. It was wonderful," Livi said as she placed her napkin on the table.

"You're welcome, sweetie. I hope you left room for the cake. I made a triple layer fudge with cream cheese icing," my mom said, and I groaned.

"Oh, stop it, it's your birthday. You'll work it off this week, I'm sure," Livi said and stood, picking up her plate in the process.

"You volunteering to help me work it off?" I asked and laughed when Livi's eyes went wide, and a pink hue formed on her cheeks.

"Lucio, behave. You're embarrassing her," my mom scolded, smacked my arm, then stood and started clearing the table.

126

I pushed my chair back and started helping. "And how did you know today was my birthday? I didn't mention it," I said and lifted a brow.

"Your mom told me when I asked if it was alright to come to dinner with you." I grinned, shook my head, and started toward the kitchen with my load items off the table. "It's polite to ask," Livi added as she followed me into the kitchen.

I sat down what I had in my hands, then took the dishes that Livi carried from her. After I stacked them, I turned to Livi, put my hands on each side of her head, bent and kissed her on the forehead.

"You are polite and sweet. And so easy to tease," I said, and as I straightened, I noticed my mom holding the cake and smiling as she watched us.

"And I have a sense of humor. So, I hope you like your gift."

"You bought me a gift?" I asked.

"I bought the material needed, but then I put it together." She smiled.

"Now, I'm curious. Let's eat the cake, Mom. I want to see my gift."

Livi handed me the wrapped box she'd retrieved from her bag. I weighed it in my hands and heard a slight rattle when I gave it a shake. I might have guessed a chain of some sort, but the box had more weight to it.

"Come on, open it," Livi said, all but bouncing in her seat.

I tore the paper off, then lifted the lid. When I

127

moved the paper that covered what was inside, I frowned. It wasn't until I pulled it out and read what was written on it, in permanent marker no less, that I burst out laughing.

It was a small flashlight, like the ones that hung off a keyring, except this one, had a chain attached so it could be worn around the neck. Livi had written on it, *'My Light'* on one side and *'From the Hallway'* on the other side.

"You're a nut," I said and handed it to my mom so she could read what was written on it.

"Well, it is sort of fitting," she said and laughed, too.

My mom knew what it represented. She found out about Livi's and my connection from Mr. Chambers the following morning when she showed up for work.

"Put it on," Livi goaded.

"Not happening," I said, and then she pouted. Even knowing it was an act, I slipped the chain over my head and let the flashlight rest against my chest. *"You're doomed,"* Tao's voice echoed in my head. There was a good chance my friend was right.

As my mom fixed me a to-go bag, Livi excused herself, leaving my mom and me alone in the kitchen.

"You're different around her, Lucio," she said, keeping her voice low so Livi wouldn't overhear.

"What?"

She looked up at me and smiled. "You're

different around her; relaxed, softer around the edges, happier. I think she's good for you."

I didn't get a chance to respond, Livi walked back into the room. Then shortly after, we were pulling away in my car.

"I had a nice time. Thanks for inviting me."

"You're welcome, and I'm glad you enjoyed yourself. Do you need to get home right now?" I asked. I was enjoying being around her, and I wasn't ready for it to end. I wanted to talk with her, learn more about her, kiss her.

"No."

"Where do you want to go? A park, the movies?" Though I wouldn't get to talk with her, but it would be dark, and I could sneak kisses from her. I'll even take you to get ice cream if you want, and I won't complain about having to watch you eat it."

"God, no ice cream. I'm stuffed. Would you mind if we went to your place? I'd love to see where you live," she said and placed her hand on my thigh.

If it'd had been any other woman who placed her hand on my thigh, I would have taken the gesture as an invitation for more. But from the little time I'd been around Livi, I got the sense she was naïve to some point. And there laid the problem. It was all on me to hold back and not push. I didn't want to pressure her or rush either one of us into something we'd regret. But, God, did I wanted her.

Chapter Fourteen

Olivia

Lucio's apartment was small but surprisingly clean for a young guy who lived alone.

"That's all of it," he said as we walked back into the living room.

"I like it. I can't wait to get a place of my own. I'll have to wait until after I graduate and get a job. Preferably an orchestra job, but I'm minoring in Education in case that falls through."

"Is it hard to get into an orchestra?"

"Oh, yes. Positions don't open very often, and they're broken down into sections: violin, like I play, viola, cello, and those are only string instruments. The hours put into rehearsing can get annoying. But the musicians and the different types of instruments playing in harmony, it's beautiful. There's no sound like in the world."

"You're passionate about it?"

"Yes, it's all I've ever wanted to do. I've dedicated a lot of time to playing the violin. I guess you could call it my gym."

Lucio stepped closer to me. "Minus the smell of sweat," he said, and I chuckled.

"Not sure if that's accurate. Playing demanding musical pieces during a ballet or opera. The orchestra pit gets a tad smelly. Especially after a few hours."

"I'm trying to be patient and attentive, but I've wanted to kiss you since I picked you up today. It's clouding my mind."

I took a deep breath and closed the gap between us. "That doesn't sound good. You should do everything to keep your mind clear," I said boldly and was feeling everything but.

"I pray you mean it," he said and grabbed my arms, pulling me against him, then leaned down to take possession of my mouth.

After the first time kissing him, if I'd never done it again, I talked myself into believing it hadn't been remarkable. Not anymore. He controlled the kiss, exploring my mouth with his tongue. When he sucked on my tongue, a shiver ran through my body.

The longer the kiss went on, the more I melted into him. I hoped his mind cleared because mine clouded. He broke from my lips only to kiss across until he reached my ear.

"I had every intention not to rush or pressure you. And I'll stick with it if you tell me that it's too

132

soon or you're not ready. But, fuck, please say yes. Please say you want me as much as I want you."

My whole life had ran on a schedule. It probably always would. I never acted on a whim or made a decision without thinking it through. Just once I wanted to throw caution away and live only in the moment. In the moment with him.

"Yes," I barely got the word out of my mouth when suddenly I was swept up in his arms, and we were moving the short distance to his bedroom. Once in his room, he set me on my feet beside his bed.

He leaned in and gave me a quick kiss, then I watched as he whipped his shirt over his head. I might have giggled when the little flashlight bounced if his body hadn't distracted me. It was absolutely the most perfect thing I'd ever seen. I'd thought I'd gotten a good look at him when he was pulling on his shirt on the other day. But staring at him now, I had gotten a portion of the time needed to appreciate what I was seeing. I could possibly stare at him for hours.

Lucio stepped forward, and I looked up at him. There was a sparkle in his eyes that hadn't been there before. He reached for my blouse and slowly unbuttoned it, sliding it over my shoulders and tossing it to the floor. Next came my bra, and he took the same care with the front hook until my breasts were freed, and the bra floated to the ground.

He made quick work of my shoes and pants,

133

and when he removed his, I briefly wondered if he would fit inside me.

"It will fit. I promise," Lucio said, and I hadn't even realized I'd spoken out loud.

Pushing me gently down onto the bed, he followed, covering me with his body. Resting on one arm, he slid the other hand up my chest. He curved his hand under my breast as his thumb moved over my hardened nipple. I arched my back when Lucio leaned forward and sucked my nipple into his mouth. His tongue left a trail of dampness as it made a circle around the nipple, and when he moved to the other, the air hit where his warm mouth had been, and my nipple hardened more.

I moved my hands and touched his back, running them up and over his broad shoulders, then down his back again. His skin was smooth and soft, but underneath I felt his toned muscles.

My back arched as he bit down none too gently on my other nipple, then licked the sting away with his tongue. He kissed up until he reached my mouth, then kissed my lips softly. When he lifted his head, and his eyes met mine, I got lost in the familiarity of their darkness.

"Livi, you are perfect."

"So are you," I answered and reached up and ran my fingers through the short hair on the sides of his head, then I pulled him down until our lips touched. I started the kiss, but he took over and consumed me. The kiss was more demanding, leaving me breathless. While our tongues dueled, he ran a hand over my ribs and my belly until he reached my center. I felt his finger as he slid it through my folds.

When he pushed the digit inside me, he released my mouth, and I gasped for air. He ravaged my breast as he pumped his finger in and out. As he added another finger, a tingling began, but as quickly as it was there, it was gone with the removal of his fingers.

There was a popping sound as he released my breast. "I can't wait to taste you," he whispered, then flicked my nipple with his tongue. "I hope you're ready to amp it up a notch."

I didn't even get a chance to respond. Lucio pushed his two fingers back into my overheated center. If not for his weight on top of me, I would have risen from the bed.

As he fingered me, he used his thumb to work my clit. My hips moved as I tried to get him to move where I needed him. With the pressure on my clit and the pumping of his fingers, the tingling returned. It took no time to feel as if I was going to explode. When I felt my core clench, its action was felt through my whole body.

"Come on, Livi, give it to me, babe," he said.

I did as he asked. My body quaked as he continued to use his fingers. "Lucio," I said when my center was left with nothing but the ending flutters of the best release of my life.

Lucio lifted his head again and looked at me. I saw a mixture of desire and satisfaction in his eyes.

To know he felt the same as I did was a heady sense of power. He removed his fingers and reached over the bed to the table. He opened a drawer and reached inside, pulling a condom out.

When he sat back on his legs, I was able to watch as he tore the square open and rolled the content down his impressive erection.

I reached out and wrapped a hand around him to see if it felt as hard as it looked. His intake of air had me shifting my eyes to his face. His face was hard, and his eyes dark.

"I'm at the last of my patience. I need inside you," he said through gritted teeth.

My response was to spread my legs wider. And it was all Lucio needed. I might have let out a tiny yelp, surprised by the speed of his actions.

He grabbed my left leg and brought it to his hip, where he held it as he leaned forward. He pushed against my entrance, and with the help of my previous release, he worked his way in. Thrusting in and pulling out until he was fully seated inside me.

The pressure his size caused was only felt until he started moving. I lifted my hips to meet his downward thrust. The rhythm he set was fast and hard and wonderful.

I didn't think he could get any deeper, but he proved me wrong when he pulled out, flipped me to my stomach, and lifted my hips. My face was pressed into the mattress by the force of his reentry. He leaned over my back and held himself up with one arm while he placed the other arm around me, flattening his palm between my hipbones.

He increased his speed, riding me hard and fast. How he was able to keep up the pace, I didn't know. But I was thankful for it just the same.

"I don't want this to end, but fuck, I'm close." With his words, he adjusted the hand on my stomach until his middle finger came in contact with my nub.

The familiar tingling began to rise inside me. As I started to fall apart, Lucio thrusted a final time. Staying buried deep inside my body as we rode the waves of our releases together.

When I finally was coherent enough to think, I was laid out on my stomach with Lucio beside me on his back. He turned his head in my direction.

"I knew you were going to be trouble for me. But that's okay, I'll deal with it. I'm going to get up, dispose of this condom, and grab us some water. Don't move, cause in about twenty minutes, I'm going to want to do that again."

My mouth dropped open as he jumped out of the bed and headed in the direction of the bathroom with an exuberant amount of energy. While I, on the other hand, laid unmoving and wondered if a heart could beat its way out of a chest.

Lucio made good on his declaration of more

sex in twenty minutes, and after the second round and while I ran to the bathroom, he'd grabbed us a snack and more water. And as we munched on the carrots, we talked, getting to know each other better.

I'd told him about the accident with my mom. My injuries and stay in the hospital. How hard it was in the beginning for my dad and me to adjust without my mom around.

He shared his own story. How stupid he felt for joining a gang. How his two biggest regrets were his dad dying, shot by someone he'd known. Tears came in my eyes when he'd spoken of his best friend Davis' death and the responsibility he felt because Davis followed him into the gang.

Lucio spoke of the injuries he sustained; fractured ribs, a gunshot wound, the hit to the back of his head that put him in a coma. He stayed in the hospital longer than I had. With each word, everything began to click into place for us. What nailed it? He shared what he experienced before his eyes had opened that he hadn't told anyone about before. He told me about his dad being there while he'd been in the coma, telling him he had to wake up, but he hadn't. At least no right away. Instead, he listened to the music playing, and when it ended, he opened his eyes.

"Do you really think it's possible?" I asked as we rested with our backs against the headboard of the bed and shared the bowl of tiny carrots and the bottle of water.

Lucio finished chewing the carrot in his mouth, and after he swallowed it down, he answered, "Everything fits, Livi. We were in the same hospital, and our time there crossed. Your doctor was Dr. Michaels, and so was mine. He'd been in your room listening while you played your violin. You even said that after you'd finished, a nurse interrupted and told him he was needed in another patient's room because he'd woken up." He shrugged. "I'll admit it's kinda wild when you think about it. But the timelines, everything fits like a puzzle's pieces."

"Do you realize just how much our lives have crossed in the last like six or so years? How close we were to each other without meeting? And before you say we did meet, I don't count it because if we had the opportunity then to introduce ourselves, we might have figured it out sooner."

"It wasn't our time to meet," he said, and I stared at him.

"Are you saying you believe the universe wanted us together, but it waited for your mom's car to break down to have us meet?"

"Yes. But I it's called fate."

"I see a whole other side to you," I said and giggled. Though in truth, what Lucio said made more sense than anything else. Maybe it was the reason I felt so comfortable in his presence.

"Are you making fun of me?"

"No."

He set the bowl and water on the table, then pounced and proceeded to tickle me. "I don't believe you."

"Stop! Stop! You're going to make me pee in your bed," I yelled.

He stopped, leaned back, then pulled me close, and I laid my head on his shoulder.

"We're going to have to get up so I can take you home. I want you to stay, but I know you can't, so I won't push. And not because of your dad, but you have classes tomorrow."

"And you have to go to the gym and train."

"Yes. My next fight will be scheduled for some time in the next two months. We know it will happen, just no confirmed date yet. I have to be ready when that happens."

I planted a kiss on his chest. "Of course, you need to be ready. This is your final steppingstone to the title fight."

"Damn, you were listening," he teased.

"Always. Can we sit like this for just a couple more minutes before we have to get dressed, and you drive me home?"

"Sure thing," he said, and I felt him kiss the top of my head.

After ten minutes, we'd gotten up and dressed, then he drove me home. I hadn't even closed the door, and I missed him. How do you miss someone you've only known for five days?

With the house locked up, I headed to bed. When I slid between the covers, I still couldn't come up with an answer. I only knew I missed him.

two paths *One* destiny

Chapter Fifteen

Olivia

"He's not someone I would have pictured you with."

I stopped walking and turned around at Dean's statement. It was verification he'd seen Lucio walk me to the music building doors after we'd shared lunch together. I'd been avoiding Dean these past two months because I hadn't wanted to hurt his feelings. We might have broken up, but he hadn't truly believed we were finished. However, if he said anything nasty about Lucio, I wouldn't hesitate to crush his feelings.

"I don't see why you can't."

"Come on, Olivia. Your educated and talented with a bright future ahead of you. He's here at lunchtime, wearing gym shorts and a tank. That says, no job." He rolled his eyes on the last part. "

I took a deep breath to calm myself before I lit

into Dean. "I don't recall you being so snobbish when we dated, Dean. I should just walk away because there really is no need for me to explain anything that has to do with Lucio. But I won't let anyone put him down when they know nothing about him. Especially, not you. So, here it is. He may not have chosen college, which there is a lot who don't, but he has worked his way to becoming one of the MMA fighters to beat. That's what he's chosen to do. His goal. As far as what I'm doing with him—besides his rocking body—he's one of the sweetest, caring men I know. I would never expect him to give up what he's worked toward for me—just as he won't ask me to give up what I've worked toward for him. Now, if you'll excuse me, I'd like to get to rehearsal. I have a busy weekend planned."

I swung the door open and walked inside, leaving Dean behind, literally, and metaphorically. I would never want to go back to the way things were before Lucio came into the picture.

I actually found myself smiling more. I'd finally met Tao, and he was just as Lucio described him. Walt, the gym's owner, and Lucio's manager was a no-nonsense man who had no problem saying what was on his mind.

Lucio's fight was coming up, and I wasn't sure I'd be able to sit through it, but I would try. For him.

Every day we spent together; we grew closer. Now, when I had thoughts of the future, he was always in them.

The reason we'd had lunch together was because I wouldn't see him until after the fight on Saturday. Lucio informed me, he was superstitious and that since he was on a winning streak, he couldn't have sex two days prior to a fight. Which meant he couldn't be around me because it would be too much temptation.

I'd shaken my head and laughed, and it hadn't even gotten a rise out of him. My guy believed we laid our own paths by the choices we made, and Karma, Fate, and Destiny played more prominent roles than what everyone thought.

Who was I to argue? Crossing paths had brought Lucio and I together.

When I entered the classroom, I walked to my chair and sat. I hoped when I told Lucio what I'd found out this morning, he'd chalk it up to fate, too.

"For God's sake, Livi. Sit still," my dad said beside me. I'd never been to the TD Garden, not once even though I'd lived in Boston my whole life. The place was huge, and I tried to watch people. Instead, my eyes always traveled back to the ring, where eventually, Lucio would arrive.

"Lucio will be okay, Olivia," Gina said from my other side.

"I know, I'm just nervous. I can't help it. What if Lucio gets really hurt, Gina? I mean, he's been in

145

a coma before. It could happen again if he takes a hit to the head."

"Livi, sweetie. Do you believe Lucio knows what he's doing?"

"Yes."

"Then relax and stop scaring Gina."

"Oh my God, Gina, I'm so sorry."

"It's okay, honey. I understand how hard it is. I wasn't even sure I would come today. So, we will sit here and lean on each other." Gina patted my hand.

"See, now relax, Livi."

"I'll try. But, Dad, I love him," I blurted out, looked over at Gina, then turned to my dad.

"Livi, tell me something I don't know," he said and chuckled, then put his arm around me, giving me a squeeze.

"And my boy loves you," Gina said and sniffled.

The announcer's voice came over the speakers, and I heard my dad mumble, "Thank God."

Lucio entered the ring, and I watched as he turned his head in our direction. He winked, then faced back toward the center as his opponent entered the ring.

I listened to the announcer go through his spiel with no clue what he said other than weight and height of Lucio and Lance Jackson, his opponent.

The fight started, and I watched and listened as my dad made comments throughout. I made a mental note to check online for an introductory book to the MMA. I was a good student, and I would learn the ins and outs before Lucio had another fight.

"That round was Jackson's," my dad said, and I looked over at him.

"Lucio did well. He knocked him down twice," I replied, and my dad shook his head and grinned.

The next round started, and my dad yelled, "You got this, Lucio. You've got time. Look at him. He didn't have to work out six days a week for five weeks straight to be here. You want it more, son. Now show him!"

"So, he's doing good?" I asked.

"Yes, sweetie. Lucio is holding his own."

I smiled and turned back to watch. Sometime between rounds, my nervousness left. I still understood nothing, but I felt I was improving since I didn't flinch when Lucio took a hit.

Lucio nodded at something Walt said in the corner, then he moved to the center of the ring. I watched Lucio charge the other man and wrap his arms around him, then he threw him to the mat.

"You've got him, Lucio. Keep his arms pinned." I glanced over at my dad. I'd never seen the man so into a sport.

"You're really enjoying yourself," I noted.

"Yes, yes, I am. Don't take this the wrong way, sweetie. I love listening to you play the violin. I've been to a hundred recitals and concerts, and I will gladly go to a hundred more, but—"

"Yeah, yeah, I know—it's a guy thing," I said,

cutting him off.

"Glad you understand," he replied, then turned back to the fight.

I looked over to Gina and shook my head. Then we both chuckled.

I turned back to the ring, and I realized that when I knew what to look for, it made it easy to watch. Lucio had Jackson's arms pinned beside him while Lucio was on his knees, straddling him. I moved to the edge of my seat when Lucio threw a forearm to Jackson's throat.

"You know they move with a lot of finesse," I surmised.

"Uh huh, that's what everyone likes about the sport. The finesse," my dad said, and I hadn't missed the sarcasm.

Lucio leaned forward with his forearm still across Jackson's throat. No way the man wasn't hurting. He had to feel almost choked.

"Put some shoulder strength into it. Don't give Jackson any room to move those hips, he'll buck you off!" my dad yelled and stood.

The crowd got louder when the referee bent down to get a better view. With Jackson's arms pinned and Lucio's legs on each side, it was hard for me to tell what was going on and exactly what the referee was looking so closely at.

The referee said something no one could hear. I stood but before I could ask my dad, the referee grabbed Lucio's arm and held it up. The crowd roared.

I knew what that meant—Lucio had won.

Lucio

I groaned as Livi stood naked in front of me. "Turn around and put your hands on the bed, Livi. You're going to want to hold on."

After the bout ended and the congratulations were over, I'd wanted nothing more than to get Livi to my place. Still riding from the adrenaline, I stripped her down as soon as the door closed, then I dragged her to the bedroom.

Livi visibly shuddered as she did what I asked. Her pert little ass had my hands reaching out to give the globes a squeeze. I ran one hand over her ass while I reached around with the other to flick her nub.

Damn, it was already hard and pushed out from its hood.

"Spread your legs wider, Livi. I want you to show me how wet you are for me." As I worked my finger in circles, she began to moan.

She laid her cheek on the mattress as her hips started rotating. I moved the hand from her ass to the inside of one thigh, then ran it up until it reached her entrance. I could feel the heat radiating from her. She was already getting wet. I smiled and ran a finger across the opening and watched as she continued to grow wetter before my eyes.

I slid the finger through her folds, and she sucked in a breath. She wiggled a little more, trying to get my finger where she wanted it. I pushed it into her heat, giving her what she desired.

"You like that, huh?" I asked, and she nodded. "Well, I hope you like this as well, 'cause I'm rock hard and ready to burst, and I want to be inside you when I do.

"Just do it, Lucio. I'm ready."

"I'll always give you what you need, babe." I stepped closer. Centered my shaft at her opening and pushed in. "Don't fight it, Livi. Relax and let me all the way in."

I worked myself in and out until she'd taken all of me. Pumped from my win and fueled by adrenaline, I set a pace to bring us both over.

Holding her hips, listening to her moans drew me closer to the brink. I wanted to hold off as long as possible because I knew once I released, every drop of energy would drain out of me, along with emptying my sac.

As the tingling started, I knew end was near. Holding on to one hip, as I continued to pound into Livi, I used my other hand to reach around to work her clit. It didn't take long for Livi to yell out my name. Then I rode her tremors and gave one last thrust, then emptied into her.

I pulled out and went to the bathroom to get a

warm cloth to clean her. I knew I'd been harder on her than usual.

Once I had her cleaned up and tucked in the bed, I slid in beside her. Laid down on my back and stretched.

"Now that is how to take care of adrenaline overload. Actually, I think it should be listed as a cure-all."

"It works for me," Livi said, then scooted closer, laying her head on my shoulder, and curling into me.

"You going to come to the next fight?" I asked and yawned.

She bent her head back so she could see my face. "They already notified Walt?"

"Yeah. Guess someone from Marco's camp was there. Came by the locker room while I was taking a shower. Three months. I'm going to get my shot at the belt. Walt thought they'd delay it as long as they could. It seems Marco is getting a lot of questions on whether he can hold onto the belt. He's thirty-six and thinks his experience will keep the young fighters from his door. So, he's figuring, go for it now. I just came off two big fights. My body's been abused. He'll try to take me down fast to prove I'm too young and not ready for his caliber of fighter."

"That's bullshit. Your body is in great shape."

I grinned. Livi never failed to have my back if she thought someone wronged me.

"Livi?"

"Hmm."

"I love you." She didn't answer back right away, and I glanced down to find her staring at me.

"I wanted to tell you first." She smacked my chest.

"It's not a competition. Are you going to say it?"

"I love you, Lucio. I do have something to tell you, and this I know you won't be able to say first."

"What? Your pregnant," I said, then laughed. When I felt the smack on my chest, I knew. I immediately sat us both up in bed.

"I don't believe you. You took my thunder again!"

"Are you serious? When did you find out?"

"I went to the doctor the other morning. I missed a couple days of my birth control pills in a row last month. When I missed my period, I wanted to be sure. I'm sorry. We've only been together a short time, and we've never talked about kids."

My girl could get on a roll, so I laid her back and started kissing her. I must have had some reserve energy because I hardened instantly. I slipped into her gently and celebrated the news.

I sat in the concert hall and watched as Livi worked the violin in her hands. Her face showed how much she loved playing it. I don't think I ever grasped how talented she was until then.

152

I might have gone to support her as she'd done with me. But I actually enjoyed myself.

Livi and I were like a coin—two sides and each different, but they were melded together.

After the symphony was over, I waited for her. When she saw me, I opened my arms and she walked into them.

"You're the flawless side of the coin," I said as I held her under one arm and took her violin case with the other.

"Is this where I say, I see a whole other side of you?"

"Nah, I only got one side. What you see is what you get, babe."

"You do not just have one side. Trust me. You have a front that I love and a backside to die for."

"I'm glad you approve," I said as we walked out.

"You know how you say that after a fight, you ride the adrenaline?"

"Yeah."

"I have some adrenaline I need to work out."

I laughed and dropped the arm I had around her and grabbed her hand. Then I prayed there wasn't a shit ton of traffic heading in the same direction of my place.

two paths *One* destiny

Chapter Sixteen

Lucio

Almost a year it'd taken me to get to this last fight that would put me on top. I listened as the only sound in the room came from the tape Tao pulled from the roll before he wrapped it around my hands. There were only three of us in the room, it was how I liked it. The quiet before the storm. I sat on the table with my focus set. Then ran through every move I would use, either to advance on my opponent or block the assault on me, along with everything else I had learned along the way. I reminded myself where I came from, where I wanted to go, and how I had gotten to this point. Hard work and the aspiration to *be* better led me on this path. Still, I wasn't sure without the support of others and their belief in me, if skill would have been enough.

The knock on the door signaled it was almost

showtime. It brought me out of my head and back to everything going on around me. Tao tossed the tape to the side and picked up my gloves.

"You're ready, Lucio. It's your time, man. I can feel it. You only have to grab it."

I nodded as Tao placed the gloves on my hands and tightened them at my wrist. He and Walt had been the ones to help me get to this level. It hadn't been easy. But from where I was sitting now, it proved with the right mindset and the motivation to strive to be the best. Anything was possible.

With the gloves on, I rotated my wrist, then brought my fingers in tight to make sure they were fitted and comfortable. As we exited the room and headed down the hall, the quietness followed until we pushed through the doors. The sold-out crowd stomped, clapped, cheered, and some even booed. It made no difference to me; I was where I was meant to be. I could only hope that when the final bell rang, there would be a new champion. Me.

The walk to the ring was different this time because it meant my effort and time climbing the ranks had paid off. I would never forget what this walk stood for.

Tao moved and held the ropes apart, and I leaned between them to enter the ring. The lights were bright, and the sound in the arena was deafening. I'd worked hard and long, spent countless hours training, and a few years to get to this point.

I shifted from foot to foot and punched the air

in front of me while I waited for the current champion to make his appearance. When the crowd became louder, I didn't even have to look to know he was making his way to the ring, they gave that away as they cheered and chanted his name.

Once Marco Turner arrived in the ring with his trainer and manager at his side, it was the first time I looked directly at him. The man wore what I had come for, the MMA heavyweight championship belt. I'd let him enjoy the moment as he unhooked the belt and turned circles while he held it over his head. He worked the crowd, and I worked to reach the peaceful place in my mind. I knew when I reached it, I felt it wash over my body.

The referee entered the ring and stepped to the center with the announcer. As the stats were given on both my opponent and me, I took that time to scan the seats. My eyes stopped on the woman who was seated off to the side. Livi sat with her dad and my mom. Her hand rested on her shirt, covering her still flat stomach. Her brown eyes met mine, and she smiled. The woman was my life. Because of her, I stood with my dream in reach. She was my motivation. She made me strive to be better. For Livi, I would do anything.

Her lips moved, and though I couldn't hear the words, I knew exactly what she mouthed as she moved her hand and placed it over her heart, "My light." It was what she called me after she realized I had been the one to collide with her and the first one she saw when her eyesight came back. Fate

157

had worked hard over the years to bring us together, and our story was still being written.

What Livi didn't realize, but what I tried to show her every day, was that she was *my light* and had been the moment I'd been touched by the music she made and brought me out of the darkness. Where would either of us be if our paths hadn't crossed?

She was now what drove me to make it to the top.

Called to the center of the ring, I touched fists with the man in front of me, and then we broke apart. It was time. My time. With the calm settled over me, I placed my focus on Marco.

I had a dream to obtain. The course of my life had brought me to this point, and I had no plans to let anyone keep it from me.

The only thing standing between me and the belt I wanted to covet was Marco Turner and five rounds, five minutes each. The arm of the referee dropped, and my single goal of being the champion started.

I charged Marco, coming in low to gain an advantage. When I was close, I reached out, wrapped my arms around him, dumping him to the mat, then landing on top of him. Marco's hips lifted, and his back arched as he rolled from side to side until finally with a buck of his hips, he'd knocked me off.

Back on our feet, we circled one another until Marco threw a couple of punches. He landed consecutive blows to my body, one to my cheek and the other on my side. I adjusted my stance and was able to block the next punch he threw, minimizing the effect as it grazed my shoulder.

I countered with my own set of punches and followed with a kick to Marco's ribs. Before I knew it, round one was over as quickly as it started, and I moved to my corner.

"You're doing great, Lucio. He's feeling that kick to the ribs," Walt spoke while I drank water from the bottle Tao had handed me.

I took the rag Walt offered and wiped my face down before I said, "He would have cut my cheek wide open if that blow had landed full force. I can still feel the sting from the fucker." I took another big gulp and let the water slide down my parched throat.

Five minutes may not sound like a long time, but in the ring as your body absorbed blow after blow and with the exertion put forth, takes an unmeasurable toll on the body.

"Just a scratch," Tao said as he leaned in to look the area over, and before I could reply to him, it was time for round two. I stood and moved back to the center with my desire and adrenaline leading the way.

Marco led the next round off with a kick that was going to leave a nice sized bruise on my thigh. I kept my balance, though it stung like a motherfucker, then I swung my leg and returned the favor. My kick landed on Marco's hip and threw him enough off balance that he had to battle to gain it back before he went down. Taking advantage, I shifted to the side and kicked out, landing the blow to the center of his chest. He hit the ropes and bounced back, then fell to his knees onto the mat. As I moved in, he pushed up to his feet and tried to sweep my feet out from under me in the process. When I jumped back, he moved forward. We both threw punches, each of us trying to gain the advantage until the second round ended.

"I'd say that round was yours, Lucio. You're better than him. Quicker. I'd even give you the first round. Focus on getting the job done and stop dancing around with him. He isn't some chump. He wants to hold on to that belt as much as you want to take it," Walt said as Tao handed me the bottle of water and I drank, then gave it back.

"He might want to keep the belt, but tough shit. It's mine." I bounced to my feet, ready to get round three started.

"Then quit playing and finish him," Walt said and stepped away.

During round three, Marco and I took turns hitting the mat. He kicked, and I performed a single leg sweep, catching him off guard and took him down. I landed on top of him and followed up with a few decent blows before he worked his hips and tossed me off.

I stepped back to prepare for a roundhouse I'd set up for my next move, but before I could complete it, Marco grabbed me from behind and placed us both onto the mat. I knocked him off before he administered more than one blow. But the blow had caught my already abused cheek, and I knew the skin had split open that time.

Back on our feet, I rushed Marco, taking away his opportunity to get set. I threw one punch after another, driving him back as he blocked the blows. Finally, I caught an opening when he dropped his hand, and with my swing, I came in contact with the brow above his left eye, and the skin opened wide. Other than bleeding from different areas of our faces, the rest of the round, we stayed relatively even. Punches and kicks, some landing, some only reaching air.

Tomorrow our bodies would be sore. But for now, the adrenaline kept us going and kept the blood pumping through our veins. The third round ended, and there was no way to call it. Our performances were equal. Marco and I had each spent ample time on the mat. We landed approximately the same number of punches and kicks. When the round ended, we walked to our corners, each with blood on our faces.

"Cuts not bad. Barely bleeding," Tao said as he patted my cheek with a towel. "But the bruising around the split is going to be nasty as it goes through the colors."

For the first time since the fight started, I glanced to the side and found Livi's eyes on me. She smiled, then blew me a kiss. I winked, then

161

grimaced when the move wrenched the skin on my bruised cheek.

"Can you put your attention back on the task at hand and off your girl? You can flirt with her later. Still can't believe you caught that young woman. You'd be smart to keep her and lock her down before she comes to her senses," Walt said as he grabbed my chin and moved my face back and forth.

"Neither can I. I know I'm a lucky bastard, and I'm not ashamed to admit it. I'm not going to let her go."

"Then you better do something about it," he answered as he fingered the skin around the 'scratch' as Tao called it. If it hadn't hurt, I would have chuckled. She was already tied to me. She'd been worried when she told me she was pregnant that I would be upset. Not a chance. It was as if the next chapter of our lives was starting, and the baby was part of it. We hadn't shared the news with anyone yet. I wanted to wait. Or until tomorrow because hopefully by the end of the night, I'd have everything, and our story would finish with a happy ending if she agreed to marry me.

"Can I at least get the fight over with first?"

Walt smacked my shoulder and snatched the bottle of water Tao had previously shoved in my hand from me.

"By all means, ride that luck and get in there and win this damn fight," Walt said, and Tao snorted.

I looked across to Marco and his trainer, who was working on getting the brow bleed to slow, and I knew. "I'm going to win. I can feel it. I just wish..."

"That your dad was here?" Tao finished for me, and I nodded. He knew my history, so did Walt.

"Who says he's not, Lucio? But—"

"But?" I questioned before Walt finished, cutting him off.

"He'd be proud no matter the outcome because you've worked and trained to be where you are. You didn't let your past dictate your future. Not everyone has the fortitude to push themselves. You were a kid who made bad choices. Now go show everyone else what I've known since the first day you stepped into the ring at my gym," Walt said, then took a step away from the ropes.

"What's that?" I asked as I stood for the beginning of the next round.

"One day, you would be a champion," Walt said and squeezed my shoulder. "Be nice if you could prove me right today."

"I agree with Walt. Now quit dicking around and do it," Tao said and stepped out of the ring with Walt.

I took as step toward the center of the ring, then stopped and I glanced over my shoulder at Tao and Walt, and they both grinned. Shaking my head, I turned and walked the rest of the way to the middle. Win or lose, the support and love from the people around me would always be there.

Of course, I would prefer to win.

The fourth round started, and Marco aggressively came at me. The consecutive punches he threw, I was lucky to have blocked them. Silently thanking all the time spent using the speed bag.

Next came a kick, which made contact with the outside of my thigh and had me staggering. The blow wasn't hard enough to take me down, but it had me fighting to keep my balance. Once my balance was under control, I advanced. Marco was ready when I kicked out from my side, and he countered. His kick landed at the back of my knee buckling it and taking me down. Straddling my back, he grabbed my arms to halt any hopes of pushing up while he went for the pin. With my arms trapped at my back, he pushed down with his weight, and I knew the fight would be over at the end of the count if I gave up now.

I rocked my hips and gained no purchase with the way his legs were positioned on the outside of me.

"Come on, Lucio! Show him who the belt belongs to. Toss him off!" I wasn't sure how Livi's ordinarily soft voice reached my ears, but it had.

"It's almost over, Moretti. You'll never be good enough to take the belt from me," Marco said, speaking for the first time during the bout as the referee began the countdown. Later, he'd kick his own ass for opening his mouth.

"The only part of that statement that's true is

164

it is almost over," I said through gritted teeth as I squeezed my eyes shut and arched my back as far as I could extend. The move raised my chest off the mat, and though the strain on my body was almost more than I could handle, I knew it was only temporary.

As the referee hit seven in his countdown, Marco adjusted his weight forward to push the top part of my torso down. The move cost him. When the weight on my hips lightened, I opened my eyes and took advantage of Marco's mistake. I used my legs to tilt to the side, which caused him to slip from my body.

Marco tried to hang on, but as the referee hit eight, I tossed Marco the rest of the way off. Once he released my arms, so he could try to scramble to get me to stay down, I pushed to my knees and was on my feet. The referee stopped his count and stepped back.

While Marco rose to his own feet, he watched my movements. I would recall the look on his face for days. Wasting no more time, I went after him. I delivered one blow after another with an intensity I hadn't had before.

With most of my punches landing, my onslaught had blood flowing from his lips and nose. Unaware of how much time was left in the round, but wanting it over, when Marco swayed, I backed away just enough and completed a one-eighty kick. The move allowed my foot to make contact under his arm. The power behind it caught him off guard and knocked him off balance, allowing me the seconds I needed to move in.

Wrapping my arm around his neck, I placed him in a 'V' hold. Applying pressure, which stopped the flow of blood to his brain, it wouldn't take long for Marco to lose consciousness.

"You might need to rethink the comment about me not being good enough to take the belt from you," I said close to his ear. "Because it is mine."

Though Marco grabbed my arms in the hope of loosening my hold, it was a wasted effort. Within milliseconds he tapped out, giving me the win by submission.

When we both stood in the center of the ring, and my arm was lifted as the new champion, I didn't think anything would ever top the feelings I had at that moment.

At least that was what I thought until I held the belt in my one hand and my other hand curved around Livi's waist after Tao had helped her enter the ring and cleared a path to me.

"I knew you could do it, Lucio," Livi said as she looked at me and smiled.

In her eyes, I saw everything—the life we would share—the children we would have together.

"Baby, with you beside me, I can do anything," I said, bent my head and captured her lips.

Fate had brought her to me.

She was my home.

She was my destiny.

two paths *One* destiny

Epilogue

Lucio

Today marked the tenth anniversary of the loss of my dad. I laid in bed with my arm draped over Livi. My hand splayed on her protruding stomach where our child nestled, then waited for the familiar weight of regret to settle on my shoulders as it had done in the past. Then again when the anniversary of Davis' death rolled around.

It didn't come, which I wasn't sure why I expected it to. It hadn't happened in a couple of years, yet I continued to wait for it to reappear.

The tiny kick against my hand brought a smile to my face. It seemed my daughter sensed my thoughts and decided to remind me that somewhere in between the dates of the worst two days of my life, she would be making her appearance.

I gently rubbed my hand in circles to try to

settle her movements, but instead, she kicked again. This time the movement had Livi shifting. I lifted my hand away so she could roll to her back. When I rested my hand back on her belly, she placed hers on top of mine and squeezed.

"I believe your daughter has her days and nights mixed up," Livi said sleepily.

I chuckled. "Oh, I see how it's going to be. She'll be my daughter when she's unruly."

I shifted to my back as Livi turned toward me. She laid her head on my shoulder while her belly rested against me. No sooner than she settled in, I received a kick to my side.

It was Livi's turn to chuckle. "Yes, she is," she replied and patted my chest.

I took my hand from her stomach and used it to run my fingers through Livi's hair. "I'm not sure you should play in the concert next week."

"I'll be fine. I have almost a month before my due date. After this performance, I'm out on maternity leave anyway."

I couldn't be prouder of Livi. She was accepted to the Boston Symphony Orchestra six months after auditioning. Her dreams had come true, too.

"I know I don't say it enough, but I'm proud of you, babe." I kissed the top of her head.

"You do tell me and show me. You will always be my light, Lucio."

"Ha! You're the one who brought me from the darkness first." I chuckled and grabbed her hand when she pinched my chest. I figured we would be going back and forth over who was whose light when we were old and gray.

"What time is it?" she asked.

Reaching to the nightstand, I lifted my phone to check the time. "Five fifty-two."

"Ugh, you know who's going to be—" Before Livi got a chance to finish her sentence, a voice shouted through the monitor.

"Mommy. Mommy. Mommy!" Each time our son called out for her his voice grew louder.

"I'll get up with him. You get some more sleep," I said, and after Livi scooted over, I got out of bed. After grabbing my pants off the chair, I headed to the bathroom to take care of my business before I took care of Joey's need. Joey was short for Joseph. We had named him after my dad.

"Thanks, honey," Livi said on a yawn as I pulled the bedroom door open.

"Anything for my girls." As I walked out, I'm not even sure she heard me before she had started to doze.

Once in the hallway, I slid the door closed as quietly as I could and made my way to Joey's room where I could hear him rattling the side of the bed. When I reached the doorway, he started bouncing in place and smiling. It never failed to amaze me how much he looked like me. He was the splitting image with his brown hair and deep brown eyes.

"Daddy!"

"Yeah, you got me this morning, buddy. We're

going to let Mommy sleep a little longer while we fix breakfast."

"Pancakes!"

"Sure thing. Let's get you to the bathroom." It had been hit and miss with potty training, but he would get there. Livi had high hopes we wouldn't have two in diapers.

"Poop," he informed me, and I couldn't help but chuckle. Seemed I was a little too late in getting to him.

"Pretty sure the smell gave you away." I grabbed what I needed and got to work. "Guess who's coming today?" I asked to keep him occupied. If not, it would take longer to get him changed.

"Grammy?"

"Yes, Grammy. She'll be here around lunchtime." Every year on the date my dad died, my mom and I spent the day together.

"Grammy candy."

I shook my head. "Yes, she always brings you candy." I lifted him out of his bed, and he yelled, "Mommy!"

"I thought you were sleeping," I said over my shoulder as I reached for the dirty diaper.

"Your daughter changed that."

"Still moving around. Maybe some food will settle her down. Little man wants pancakes." I turned to face Livi, and she rubbed her belly as she blew out her breath in short bursts.

"Oh, shit. Now?"

"Shit!" was repeated by Joey, and even in pain, my wife cocked her brow.

"Sorry. Let me get my phone, and I'll call Mom and tell her we need her to come now."

"Done. I did it before I even got out of bed. She said she'd be right over."

"Okay, good. The contractions just started, so we got a few hours. It took twenty-four hours before Joey was born. But she is early, though."

"About that. I might have been in labor yesterday evening when I thought the tiny contractions were Braxton Hicks. They're five minutes..." her water broke and ran down her legs, hitting the floor, "apart."

I sat in the hospital chair, holding Lucia Constance Moretti, my daughter, and watched my wife as she slept.

At twenty-six, I'd exceeded my dream of success in the MMA. I had a talented wife, two kids, money in the bank, and a home in the suburbs.

I'd learned it was okay to fail as long as you didn't give up. Life came without a manual or warranty and needed to be lived as if there was no tomorrow. It wasn't to say I wouldn't have more regrets over my lifetime, I just refused to let them define me.

I was living proof there was more than one path to follow.

Livi's and my relationship was fast. Most would view it as an insta-love story. When actuality, it was so much more.

Two young people whose lives crossed at different points until it was time for us to meet. The story had been in the making for almost seven years—it just waited for Livi and me to grow up enough to put all the pieces together.

We've gotten off to a good start, but our story is long from finished.

Acknowledgments

Thank you to everyone who has followed me on my writing journey. Your support has and is much appreciated. You make the hours sitting in front of the computer worth it.

Carson

two paths *O*ne destiny

About the Author

Carson Mackenzie enjoys writing romance with a real feel inside the stories. She writes with the belief not every man is a jerk and not every woman needs saving.

Carson lives in the South with her son, a Great Dane and two adopted shelter dogs that keep the household in line. Books have always been a part of her life. There is nothing better to her than curling up and relaxing with a good story and losing herself in someone else's world for a few hours.

Writing stories and growing as an author with each book is her goal. She wants to reach the level where a reader knows when they see her name on a cover, they can trust in the fact there will be a good story as they flip through the pages.

Carson's journey into writing has only been for a few years. As she's finally starting to settle in, she can't believe she waited so long to start.

To stay up to date with Carson – you can follow on her website and sign up for her Newsletter.

Books by Carson Mackenzie

Black Hawk MC

Speed
Crusher
Devil
Ghost
Jag
Coast
Flirt
Flyboy & Preacher - TBA

Boxed Sets

Black Hawk MC Books 1-3

Haven MC

Snatched
Hawk's Bounty
Keg's Revelation
Crank's Bombshell - TBA

Desert Phoenix MC

Irish's Resolve

Standalones

Her Way or No Way
two paths One destiny

two paths *One* destiny

www.ingramcontent.com/pod-product-compliance
Lightning Source LLC
Chambersburg PA
CBHW030158200626
46812CB00017B/2695